Broken Wing

SHERELLE WINTERS

Zenbi Press

Zenbi Press
1511 Texas Avenue S #325
College Station, Texas 77840-3328

ISBN 978-1-949055-04-7

Library of Congress Control Number: 2019905296

First Printed 2019

Chapter 1

A LIGHT FOG DANCED IN front of pale headlights as the sun painted the sky's edges a dusky blue. During the long night, the farmlands of Tennessee and rural North Carolina had given way to the state's iconic pines; they lined both sides of the highway like silent sentries, breaking only for the occasional water crossing or exit ramp.

Tucking her long hair behind her ear, Jessie Bradshaw pressed the button to open the Honda Pilot's panoramic roof. The breeze perfumed the car with the clean, crisp scent of the trees. She hadn't realized how much she'd missed that beloved smell until it filled the car. A sigh of contentment escaped her.

From behind her, a large, furry head rested on the SUV's center console. With a barely stifled yawn, Jessie gave her a quick pat. "Good morning, girl, or close enough anyway. Doing okay back there?" Weighing in at 140lbs, Jessie knew the Caucasian Shepherd had to be getting cramped on the back seat, especially considering how long they had been on the road, but she'd handled it like a champ, alternating between watching out the windows and napping on the bench seat.

The classic country song by George Strait faded on the radio as the local morning show started up. Jessie reached over to turn it down as the two nauseatingly energetic DJs bantered with one another while sharing news and joking about the latest viral video. She debated looking for another station but figured they were all doing the same start up routine and she'd be out of luck getting a station that stuck to mostly music for the last part of her trip. It made her wish, not for the first time, she'd paid for the subscription to the music-on-demand service the Pilot could have come with, but at the time, she hadn't seen any need for it.

The headlights flashed on a green highway sign. Sixty miles to Asheville, where she'd leave I40. Then it was another eighty miles of smaller highways and back-roads before home would finally be in sight. While the darkness hid her from the world better, Jessie was glad the last part of the drive would be at a time when the deer and other night creatures returned to their sleeping spots for the day. Having to keep vigilant for the flashes of eyes near the road had been an effective sleep deterrent; she'd seen what a deer could do to a vehicle, even one as large as the Pilot.

She absently reached up to stroke the rim of her glasses, but of course they weren't there. It wasn't safe to wear them at night when they weren't needed for vision correction and had no anti-glare coatings. It was another reason she had chosen to leave Chicago in the early evening instead of making the drive during the day time. At night, rest stops were quieter, no one to see her and be bothered, not that it stopped her from putting them on before getting out. But it was rougher driving, long hours with nothing but repeating music and the highway's dangerous lullaby doing its best to sing her to sleep. Even with the stretch breaks, more coffee than she'd ever admit to drinking, and regularly opening the window to let in some cold air, the drive was starting to take its toll.

"Okay, girl, looks like we'll be home in two, maybe three hours! You're going to like it there, I'm sure. Way better than that tiny hotel room and grass area. I mean, you were a good girl there, don't get me wrong, but I know you had to feel so cooped up! The house has a couple acres of land for you to roam, you'll be much happier there." As if she understood every word, Causy thumped her fluffy cream and gray tail on the backseat. Sometimes Jessie wondered how much of her babbling the dog understood. She'd been talking out loud to her since she'd gotten her as a puppy, and the canine often reacted as if she was sagely listening and absorbing every word.

As the highway wound its way into Asheville, Jessie spotted a restaurant marker noting her favorite regional breakfast chain at the next exit. Her mouth watered and she bit her lip at the thought of a good southern breakfast. She could almost smell it from the highway. It had been at least three years since she'd had a meal from Biscuitville. It was as good a time as any to make a pit stop being still early enough for blessedly little traffic at the drive-through.

But there was still the person at the window. They would see her, even with the glasses, which didn't wrap around her whole face, and the tinted windows, which would have to be lowered to get the food. What if it happened again? She felt herself shaking at the thought and finally pulled into the parking spot furthest from the building to calm down.

Causy whined and moved her head to Jessie's shoulder, gently nuzzling her with a wet nose. "I know girl, I know. I just…I can't. I know I'm a coward. I'm sorry. We'll get out and stretch at a rest stop, I promise. But here, I just can't. I'm sorry."

The shaking finally stopped, and Jessie pulled back on the road. She continued driving through town until she was back in the quiet of the woods. As promised, she stopped at the first rest stop she found and let Causy out to potty. The early morning light sprinkled through the trees as Jessie scanned the area for signs anyone else was around. Satisfied the drivers of the two tractor trailers in the stop were asleep in their cabs, she called Causy to her. "C'mon girl," she said as she headed to the women's bathroom. Even if no one else was around, she wasn't about to go into an isolated space without the big dog with her. She jumped at the sound of a twig breaking, but as Causy didn't react, she told herself it was just a night critter startled by her footsteps.

When she returned to the Pilot, she opened the hatchback and raided the cooler to grab a Dr. Pepper, sandwich, and some fruit. It was a far cry from the fluffy biscuit with perfectly cooked sausage patty or the hot bowl of cheesy grits she could be enjoying, but it was something. Causy sat beside her and looked up at her, but like the well-trained dog she was, she waited patiently. With a smile, Jessie reached into a box, giving her a handful of large dog biscuits.

For twenty-nine years, she'd been a regular woman who was able to do normal things like eat out and go shopping, but now thanks to *him* she was a coward who couldn't even manage a drive-thru. It was a minor miracle she'd gotten in the car and driven as far as she had, helped by knowing that other drivers wouldn't see her enough to notice the scars or if they somehow did see her, she couldn't see their reactions much less be afraid of them.

Just after nine in the morning, they finally reached the small, often overlooked town of Cascade Falls. Jessie drove through downtown, barely noticing the familiar buildings due to the alarming frequency of her yawns. It was with no small amount of relief she spotted the white fence marking the edge of her grandfather's property. The sight of the dusty pink two-story house flooded her with memories of childhood romps through the old house, enjoying lemonade and swinging on the wrap-around porch's swing, and running through the surrounding fields during the summer.

A renewed sadness at her grandfather's passing burned in her chest. As she drove down the small gravel driveway, her sadness only increased when she saw how shabby the house looked. The porch was sinking in one corner and there were several balustrades missing. The once stately columns on either side of the double front door looked more like they were barely keeping the weight of time from collapsing the entire structure.

"Oh Causy, the old girl is really showing her age, isn't she?" Causy stuck her head out the back window, staring at the house as if evaluating its appearance before giving a gruff bark. Chuckling softly, Jessie drove up the long drive, parking as close to the front of the house as she could without pulling into the overgrown grass. "Alright girl, this is our home now. What do you say we head inside and get some sleep? We can unpack later."

Jessie grabbed one of the suitcases from the back and locked the SUV. The warped wooden steps creaked as she made her way to inside. The smell of lemon and pine filled the air. The cleaners James hired to go through the house the day before appeared to have done an excellent job airing it out. While time had laid its never ending hand on the inside as well, with the creaking steps and floors, it still felt clean and warm.

With a small smile, she gave Causy a pat. "We're finally home, girl." The vigilant dog stayed close at her heels, sniffing thoroughly as they entered and walking with the stiffed gait of being at high alert. After a few minutes, seeming satisfied it was a safe place, the dog relaxed and assumed a more natural posture.

Not that Jessie felt any fear. Even with signs of the house being cleaned, there was a hollow feeling to the place. It had been months since her grandfather passed, and his absence was palpable as she made her way up the stairs to the second floor. Having no desire to deal with seeing her grandfather's things or such personal memories yet, Jessie passed the master bedroom and headed to the guest room.

Dropping her suitcase by the door, she headed into the small, attached bathroom, whipped back the powder blue shower curtain, and turned the faucet to get the water warming. She knew it would take a minute or two for the hot water to reach the pipes up here. Once the steam started, she turned on the cold and got the water to a comfortable temperature. With exhaustion weighing down her limbs, she kept the shower brief, just enough to wash away the long drive.

The bed was bare, so she headed to the living room, too tired to deal with making the bed. As she expected, the pink and blue afghan she'd given Grandpa years ago was tossed on the sofa, no doubt by him one evening before going to bed, maybe even during his last evening alive. Picking up the beloved old blanket, Jessie held it close, taking in the comforting scents of family and home. She felt herself tearing up and she took several deep breaths. "We can fall apart later. Sleep now."

With that determined statement, she lay on the sofa and cried herself to sleep.

Chapter 2

A DEEP, MENACING BARK jerked Jessie from sleep. She scrambled up from the sofa. Glasses firmly in place, she headed to the partially open front door. Sometimes too smart for her own good, Causy had long ago figured out how to open almost any unlocked door and even a few locked ones. As tired as Jessie had been when they arrived, she didn't remember throwing the bolt on the old door before falling asleep.

As she reached for the handle, a man's voice came from the yard. She froze in her tracks. The tremors were instantaneous. She curled her hands into fists, unable to control them. Causy barked again. Jessie shook herself from the trance long enough to pull the door open a smidgen further, just enough to peek around it into the yard. Causy's massive body was halfway down the drive, head down, hackles raised. Throaty snarls filled the silence between her alert barks. Her ears flicked back a moment, acknowledging Jessie's presence.

At the end of the drive stood two decidedly uncomfortable-looking men. One was brown-haired with a white shirt and jeans. He stood just behind another man of similar coloring but wearing the royal blue Cascade Falls police uniform. It was him she watched more, as he was the armed one.

His gun was still in its holster, but he had his hand on it while keeping a watchful eye on Causy for any movement. She was glad he was following the police protocols she'd helped Julianna write on dealing with dogs, not that their local force would hire any hotshot, trigger-happy guy who would just shoot a guard dog acting like a guard dog should. Still, she knew even with training, not many people kept their composure well when a large dog stood before them.

Seeming to spot her movement at the door, the civilian said something to the other man, then gave her a shaky wave while calling out to her. "Hey there. Sorry to startle you. Great guard dog you have, but do you think maybe you could call this big fellow off so we can come up to visit?"

With only two hours of sleep from her long drive, her politeness factor was well past the point of pretending to be nice, much less being open to the idea of two strange males coming any closer to her than they already were. Ignoring his request to bring Causy in, she yelled back.

"This is private property and unless you're here on official business Officer and Mister Not-an-Officer, then you two are trespassing. I'd thank you to turn around and go back to where you came from."

This time the cop tried. "Ma'am, I'm Officer Andrews. I received a report about the car outside this house and wanted to be sure no one was up to anything here with old man Clark's place."

Biting back a snarky response, she tried to remember her manners enough to get them to go away. "Thank you for checking, Officer, but this is now my house and as such I have every right to be here. And as I have not broken any laws nor asked for your assistance, I'm asking you again to leave me alone."

The two men whispered to each other before the officer waved in acceptance. "Sure thing, ma'am. Like I said, just checking." He glanced at Causy, who was still in full protective stance.

"Go on, as long as you're leaving and ain't up to no good, she won't come after you."

Though both men nodded to show they heard her, they kept a careful eye on Causy and walked half-backward until they stepped off the property and across the road. Jessie watched them continue down the street to a large, light gray house with a truck and a police cruiser parked in front. Close enough to be good neighbors, if she hadn't been so rude to the guy she presumed lived there. Once they were out of sight, Jessie leaned against the door, taking several deep breaths to calm the last of her nerves.

Causy trotted back up the drive and into the house, tail wagging and expecting praise. Though Jessie had discouraged the door opening trick, she still praised her for guarding the house properly and tossed her a dog treat.

After seven years in Chicago, Jessie'd almost forgotten the old Southern ways of life, where neighbors would actually notice and come by to check on something like a strange car in a dead neighbor's yard. In a town like Cascade Falls, such actions weren't just common–they were expected. It was a town built by folks looking out for one another.

The town's roots began with Jessie's great-grandfather. He had come to the area in the early 1900s in search of a safe place to raise his family. Over the decades, the Bradshaw's homestead swelled with family and close friends invited to take advantage of the refuge. By the time Jessie was born, the town boasted a population of some three hundred people.

The Bradshaw clan had always done their best to care for the town and its citizens, a family responsibility ingrained in each from birth. Those who lived there appreciated their efforts.

The town had little crime, well-maintained streets, and many of the services and amenities boasted by cities multi-times their size, including well-equipped, well-trained police and fire departments, and small, but fully appointed schools competitive with the best schools in the state. At the same time, deliberate actions were made to keep the town small and avoid infiltration by chain stores, with all the businesses in town locally owned and operated. Cascade Falls was nearly autonomous in many ways, having little interference in day-to-day matters from the county, state, or even federal governments.

No doubt the police officer would check out her claim to own the house and Julian would likely call her later to fuss at her response, but she was too tired to worry about it now. All she really wanted was to go back to sleep, but she knew her body well enough to know it wasn't likely to happen anytime soon. Instead, she quickly changed to shorts and a tee-shirt, then headed into the kitchen for a cup of coffee. At which point she realized she hadn't thought to have the house stocked with food or anything else. While the town had a lot of modern amenities, she doubted they had a grocery delivery service like she'd used in Chicago.

With a heavy sigh, she gave up on getting her caffeine hit for the hour and instead went back to the front door. Even the thought of going out in the yard had trembles starting in her hands, never mind that she had no intentions of going further than the Pilot which was sitting so close to the steps it was practically in the house. With that small comfort, and after checking thoroughly to be sure no one else was lurking around outside, she opened the hatch with the key fob then darted outside to grab the remaining two suitcases. Two more exhaustive check and runs for the vehicle had three good sized cardboard boxes and the near-empty cooler in the house, which finished the task of unloading her meager belongings.

She'd only brought a few clothing items she'd ordered online just before leaving, mementos she had of her parents, a couple of special books and gifts, and of course Causy's things. The rest she'd left behind, wanting nothing reminding her of the life she'd once had in Chicago, not even the pictures of the people she'd met there and called friends. The "friends" who hadn't even come to see her at the hospital or visited after *it* all happened. The "friends" who acted as if she'd died, instead of caring she survived.

She left unpacking the boxes and suitcases for later, other than retrieving Causy's bowl so she could dish out breakfast. At least she'd prepared for one of them to eat, she thought to herself in disgust before checking the cooler one more time to see if something humanly edible had magically appeared.

She looked out the window at the Pilot again, sitting there taunting her with its mobility. There was a grocery store not even a mile away, and this was home, not Chicago. People here weren't the same as the ones there, they wouldn't act the same. But even as she tried to draw the mental image of herself driving to the store successfully, as the therapist at the hospital had suggested, she felt the tremors start again. Automatically, her hand came up to touch the rim of her glasses.

I'm such a goddamn coward. I drove from Chicago, but now I can't go to the store? People go to the store every day. So what if people stare? So what if they talk? You need food, get off your ass and go!

Option two, mentally berating herself, did not make her feet move either. With a disgusted sigh, she found her cell phone and made the call she should have made the moment she arrived.

Chapter 3

GALEN ANDREW'S SON, Michael, who had first reported the strange car at the house, was waiting in the kitchen, eager to hear about his trip to Mr. Clark's. With the excitement over, for now, Galen finished setting out their lunch then briefly explained that a woman calling herself Clark's granddaughter had taken up residence and had not been very welcoming.

"After what happened this morning, son, I think it would be a good idea for you and Kipper to stay away from Mr. Clark's place for a while. That dog was huge, and it was not friendly. It could hurt you both if it decided you were invading its territory." Galen stared at the shepherd mix puppy they'd adopted a few months ago. Kipper would about snack size to that monster dog he'd just seen. Clearly oblivious to his scrutiny and subsequent scowl, Kipper sat at Michael's chair begging for scraps.

"Aww, Dad, do I have to? I really want to meet Mr. Clark's granddaughter. He was always talking about her. I saw a picture of her once and she is really pretty. It would be nice to get to talk to her finally."

"Who are you talking about son? Mr. Clark didn't have any children or grandchildren." While he was smart for his age, Michael was still only ten so Galen presumed he must have misunderstood something. Everyone knew the old man hadn't had any family to speak of when he died, certainly no children. And if he had left the house to some stranger, the whole town would have been buzzing by now. Galen still wasn't sure if he was pissed at the squatter for her rudeness or amazed at her audacity in claiming she'd inherited Mr. Clark's house.

"Dad, of course he did," Michael answered with a slightly exasperated tone. "Like I said, he talked about her all the time. I even remember him mentioning she had some kinda huge dog as big as a pony! That's probably the one you met. I figured he had been exaggerating. Never seen a dog that big, you know? Be cool to see it. You sure it's mean?" he asked with a hopeful tone.

"I'd rather not take chances," Galen replied firmly. "For now, Uncle Phillip said to leave her be while he checks things back at the station." Then he could take a few other officers to send the rude squatter packing, safely. "That aside, I'm trying to understand how Mr. Clark can have a granddaughter without having had any children?" While most folks in the town were respectful of each other's privacy, whoever this stranger was wouldn't be considered part of the crowd, and it was still a small town after all so gossip still travelled pretty fast.

"Oh, he told me once that they don't have the same blood, but it didn't matter because they were family all the same. I didn't understand all of it, but I think he kind of meant that they were like Timmy's family. You know, he didn't come out of his mom like I came out of my mom, but they adopted him and so they are a family anyway?"

"Ah, I gotcha." Galen began clearing the dishes. "Well, for now, just stay on this side of the road for me, okay? Even if that is who is there, she didn't seem to want company and I can't trust that dog when it came growling at two full-grown men, okay?"

"Yes, sir." His disappointment was clear in his voice.

"Meanwhile, I think you have some homework that needs doing, and I need to make a call right quick."

"Okay. Come on Kipper." Michael half ran up the stairs, the pup right at his heels. Galen debated yelling after him to walk but decided to let it go. He had a feeling he was forgetting something and his conversation with Michael made that feeling even stronger. Once he finished cleaning up, he called

Phillip to share Michael's revelation about the "adopted" granddaughter.

"Hmm…you know, thinking about it, the Bradshaw clan was pretty close to him. They were all there in the front row at his funeral, well, all except the youngest, Jessie. I heard they were footing all his medical bills those last few years and covered the funeral costs too."

"That's true, but they are like that with just about everyone in town. Anyone can't afford something, they take care of it."

"Oh, I know, they helped me out when I wanted to leave Durham. Still, I vaguely remember when we used to visit here a lot as kids, Jessie was always hanging around at Mr. Clark's place instead of wanting to be with the rest of us. Hang on, I just spotted Julian, let me check with him."

While he waited for Phillip to return to the phone, Galen thought back to those childhood vacations. His grandparents had relocated to Cascade Falls while Galen was still in middle school. At first, he and his brother hated spending their summer vacations there. Having grown up in the city, they found the little "backwoods" town decidedly lacking in excitement.

As adults, they both ended up moving to Cascade Falls themselves, though, for different reasons. Phillip loved being a cop from the day he entered the academy, but he grew tired of the violence and day-to-day death he'd dealt with working in Durham. It left him feeling like he wasn't making a difference or really helping anyone. He'd been just about ready to quit altogether when he'd learned of an opening on the Cascade Falls police force. It had been a perfect opportunity, except he didn't have the funds to relocate. The Bradshaws stepped in to provide a more than generous relocation package, and the force somehow managed to give him a few weeks paid leave before he even started so he could settle in.

After Melinda's death, Galen had been lost himself, functioning only by sheer determination and the need to care for Michael and help him cope with the loss of his mom. It had been Phillip who recommended they come to Cascade Falls, suggesting the change of scenery and the excitement of starting something new could help them both heal. It had been a godsend, with Michael loving the country air and being able to play outside, and Galen had "magically" found himself having plenty of work as soon as he'd been ready to start up again. He was fairly certain the Bradshaws had a hand in it, much as they had with Phillip. Sometimes he wondered if the family was really as generous as they appeared, but he hadn't been about to look a gift horse in the mouth.

"Galen?" Phillip's voice broke through his musings. "Julian confirmed it, Clark left the house to Jessie, and she was due to move in sometime today."

"I guess that's good then. Glad the place won't sit empty and ruin. I did wonder why there hadn't been any word of an estate sale or anything."

"Yep, might mean you have to wait a few more decades to get your hands on it to restore it," Phillip teased, well aware of his brother's desire to fix the old house up. "Oh, don't forget the police dog exhibition next month. I know Michael is really looking forward to it."

"How can I? He reminds me morning, noon, and night!" Still laughing, Galen hung up and went back to cleaning the house. He wondered what Jessie's plans were for the old house. While it was no mansion, Galen loved the architectural details. It had hand carved, intricate woodwork throughout, lovely pillars and the trademark balcony running around the outside. It was just this side of being an antebellum home and had been built when the first Bradshaw had come to the area over a century ago. He longed to apply his skills to make it over, but with Clark's health declining over the last few years before his death, a major house renovation had certainly not been at the top of the priority list.

From what he could remember, the princess of the Bradshaw clan lived in a big city up north somewhere. He hadn't even heard of her being in town the last three years. More than likely she'd just sell the house and everything in it, then head home. Doing some quick mental calculations, he knew it would stretch his personal budget a bit, but he could probably afford the home at its current value, especially if Jessie wanted it sold quickly.

Presuming, of course, she didn't hate him and refuse to sell to him out of spite after their meeting this morning. He winced inwardly. While it wasn't his fault, it wouldn't do to find himself on the wrong side of the controlling family of

Cascade Falls. Thinking back again to the laughing, dark-haired girl from those long past summers, he remembered her as friendly enough, if a bit introverted. Had the big city changed her that much?   Did she remember him at all? Would she have been friendlier if they had recognized each other?

Ah well, in a town this size, they were certain to run into one another soon, at which point he hoped they could start over.

Chapter 4

"BRADSHAW." HEARING HER brother's deep voice gave Jessie comfort. James had taken on the role of head of the family after their mother's death. He'd played dad to them all, especially Jessie, who was the youngest. Growing up, James had never missed one of her plays, PTA meetings, science fairs, book fairs, or any of the other myriad of seemingly important events in a young child's life.

"James…it's me."

"Hey 'me.' I could have sworn I told you to call me when you got in?"

"I know and I'm sorry. I was so tired when I arrived, I fell asleep as soon as I stepped inside the house."

"Yeah, I figured. Fortunately, the Andrews brothers were watching the place, so I knew you arrived safe and sound."

"Andrews? That name sounds vaguely familiar."

"Remember Thomas and Corinne? They passed, oh, ten years or so ago, but they've lived in town as long as I can remember."

"Oh, yeah, their kids and grandkids visited in the summer." Jessie replied, easily slipping into the Southern ways of weaving information about people into the flow of the conversation. "Corinne always had lemonade and fresh sweets on hand when we played with their grandboys. Galen and Phillip, right?"

"That's right. Those two live here now. Phillip's in their old house and Galen is your neighbor across the way." He paused as if sensing her tension. "They're good folks, Jess. You don't need to worry about them."

"I know. I know…" She didn't need to say aloud that her fears of going out in public or of strangers were irrational; she'd already told herself repeatedly, but still, they remained. Though considering she'd threatened them both in the driveway, they might not really be considered good neighbors anymore. Not that she had any way of dealing with it, she wasn't about to walk down to apologize, not in her condition.

"So how is the house? Did the cleaning crew do alright?"

"Yep, the house is spotless. I should have had a lawn service come by though. It's horribly overgrown. Even Causy could disappear in the weeds."

James laughed at the idea. "I don't think I want to see grass tall enough to lose that overgrown bear. You know, Jack just bought himself a pretty little John Deere. I've been looking for an excuse to try it out, so why don't I come by in a bit and take care of that lawn for you, okay?"

She knew it wasn't really a question, but a statement of what he was about to do, but she still asked if he was sure it wouldn't be a bother. James balanced his time between running the town and his international security consulting firm, though he was never too busy for family.

"Of course not, sweetie. Everything else good to go?"

"Um, well…" She hesitated to say it out loud, hating to voice her cowardice. Of all her brothers, James was the one she had never known to be afraid of anything or anyone. He was strong, the rock of the family, and here she was too scared to do an everyday task.

"Come on, Lil' Bit, what's wrong?"

"There isn't any food in the house, and no matter how hard I try, I can't get myself out that door to drive to the store. Even having Causy with me, I'm afraid of seeing anyone I know or worse, that I don't know. I just…"

"Ah Jess, it's all right. You just listen to me, okay? You'll get through this, it's just gonna take time. Meanwhile, I'll bring some groceries with me when I come, okay? So dry those tears, hon, and I'll see you in a bit."

Jessie dried her eye, the only one that could produce tears anymore, as she hung up the phone before reaching down to snuggle Causy, who'd come to sit at her feet. "I hope he's right, girl. I hope we'll be okay."

She straightened and took a deep breath. "While we wait, we might as well look around the house and get ourselves settled into an actual bedroom. James will worry more if he thinks I'm sleeping on the sofa."

On the second floor, she forced herself to walk into Grandpa Clark's bedroom and tackle the memories, only to find there was nothing left to tackle. The house had apparently been cleared of most of his personal belongings already, other than the main pieces of furniture. It was a strange feeling, walking around the depersonalized room. While the bed, dresser, and side tables were the same, the room lacked the bedding, the clothes, the photographs, the little touches. It felt almost like a stranger's room.

Grandpa had never married, and while he had blood relatives, they had lost touch long ago. The heavily religious family had ostracized a teenage member of Grandpa's family for no other reason than he'd been born gay. Grandpa hadn't been willing to stand by and let it happen, so he took the boy in himself, turning his back on the rest of the family in the process.

The boy had been grateful and had been as close to a son as Grandpa ever had. But he'd been killed in his senior year of college, a promising honors graduate who'd been the victim in a botched convenience store robbery that also left the store clerk and another shopper dead. Grandpa had been heartbroken and mourned the boy for a long time.

Some wondered if he would ever recover when James had moved the rest of the Bradshaw kids back to town, following their own mom's death. Jessie had been taking it especially hard. She'd taken to wandering in the woods, which was where she'd met Mr. Clark, who had done much the same. In a way, the heartbroken old man and the little girl had helped each other heal and move on, forming a bond of shared pain that hadn't been broken by distance.

Jessie moved to the guest room she'd originally planned to use. Clean sheets were stacked in the nearby linen closet, along with blankets. Recognizing the ones that had often been on the guest bed, she selected those. "Got to follow tradition, right girl?"

Once the bed was made, she headed back downstairs to carry up the suitcases and boxes, then set about getting everything unpacked and in place.

Chapter 5

IT HADN'T TAKEN THEM too long to buy the groceries and arrive at the house. James hesitated at the stairs, no doubt remembering how she'd pulled away from him at the hospital. At the time, she'd been so terrified she'd rejected anyone's touch: the doctors, the nurses, and she'd pulled away from James when he'd arrived. Though he'd understood, she'd still seen the flash of pain at her fearing him.

Once she'd begun healing and had calmed some, she had moved past the fear, at least for her siblings and her best friend Jazza. All others' touch still startled her, and she was hesitant to reach out to anyone, male or female.

The psychologist suggested it was a subconscious response to feeling she could no longer trust her judgment about people and therefore automatically decided not to trust any of them. Not that it was a huge hindrance; she didn't see anyone but her family and Jazza anymore.

Glad she no longer had to fight irrational fears of the most important man in her life, she half ran down the stairs and into his waiting arms, sinking into the security of that familiar space. The breeze outside swished through her hair, and the warmness of his chest comforted her.

He hugged her tight and kissed the top of her head. "Welcome home, Lil' Bit."

Jack joined them, and Jessie turned to hug him as well, his grip just as firm as their older brother's.

"Hey, baby girl," Jack murmured with his trademark grin. "I hope you're hungry. I don't think James left anyone else in town a lick of food at the store. He practically bought the whole place."

"Did not." James laughed and motioned for Jessie to follow. "Come on, let's get the food in the house while stingy there mows the grass since he won't let me drive."

Jessie laughed, one of the first real laughs she'd had in a while. Everyone knew that James had a love of speed and riding in a car with him was a good way to scare years off your life. To his defense, he'd never had an accident, so while he may have pushed the speed boundaries of pretty much anything with wheels, he certainly didn't do so recklessly. But she couldn't blame Jack for wanting to keep his new mower out of his brother's hands.

After thanking Jack for taking care of the lawn, she joined James at the trunk of his large SUV. Seeing the number of bags nestled in the roomy back area, she couldn't help laughing again.

"You sure you left anything?"

"Just that nasty stuff you'd never eat anyway," James joked before picking up four of the paper sacks and heading into the house. Jessie followed behind, carrying two. By the time the car was unloaded and everything put away in the kitchen, the cabinets were practically groaning with food. The fridge barely had room for air to flow. She wouldn't need restocking for weeks, at a minimum. Her chest expanded with relief. Maybe that would be enough time for her to be better enough to attempt shopping by herself.

With the food put away, they headed back outside to sit on the porch. The front lawn was of a sensible height again, and the smell of fresh cut grass filled the air. She could hear Jack riding off to tackle the rest of the two acres surrounding the house. Though there was a cool breeze in the air, summer was trying to get in one last blast of heat, so she was glad he'd taken a bottle of water with him. It could get hot, even on a riding mower, after a long enough time.

Meanwhile, she and James sat on the creaky, but sturdy white swing on the wrap-around porch drinking iced water. He asked again how she was doing.

She'd started to say she was okay, but she knew he'd see through the lie and call her on it.

"I'm…I'm hanging in there. The drive was rougher than I thought. Couldn't even get myself to go through restaurant drive-thrus. Glad I packed the cooler or I'd have been half starved by the time I arrived here. Rest stops were easier for bathroom breaks, not too hard to find empty ones that time of night or ones where most folks were asleep. Causy discouraged anyone from getting too close if they were awake."

"Well, I'm proud of you for making it down here. It would have been easy enough for you to have me come get you in an RV like I offered, but you managed to get here on your own. Don't sell yourself short, okay?"

"Believe me, it was tempting. And yeah, I know, it will take time. At least here, it's quiet and I can manage to feel comfortable outside, like this."

"Exactly." The corners of his mouth turned up as he squeezed her hand. "Hopefully you'll be able to sleep better too."

"Hopefully. So far so good, anyway, though the short bit I slept probably isn't enough to judge. You'd think this far away my brain would realize it's okay. He's locked in a federal penitentiary, he can't get me here. But I knew he couldn't get me at the hotel either and still..." A chill ran through her. Though it wasn't logical, she kept having dreams of him somehow escaping and coming after her again.

"Don't you worry Lil' Bit. You know, no matter what, he isn't getting away with this." He held up his hand to stop her interruption. "I know, I know. I'm letting the law have their chance like you asked. But they screw up, I'll sort it out. He will never, ever get his hands on you or anyone else again."

She nodded. When she'd asked James to let the courts handle punishing Crichton, he'd argued against it. But despite what had happened, she still wanted to believe in the legal system, and she argued that if she was willing to deal with testifying, he should respect that. He'd finally relented, but still, she knew what he said was correct. Safe at home, even if Crichton somehow could escape, he would have to get through her brothers to get to her again.

Jessie suddenly remembered James standing in the hospital, crying as he held her hand and apologizing. "You know it's not your fault, right?"

"He never should have gotten his hands on you to begin with. It's my job to protect you, all my family. And I failed you."

"James, you didn't fail. If anyone did it was me. I was the one looking right at a monster and unable to see him for what he was. I did the background on him and missed any signs. And I didn't listen to you. You taught me how to protect myself, but I wrote it off as you being overprotective as usual. I…"

He pulled her against him as her voice trailed off into sobs. "No baby, no. It isn't your fault, I swear. You couldn't have known. I'm not even sure he realized what he was until it was too late, there is still nothing to show he'd done anything that would have been a warning sign before."

Jessie sniffed and returned the embrace. "I'll make a deal with you. I'll try to stop blaming myself if you do too. If I couldn't have known, how could you?"

He snorted. "Nice turn around, smart aleck." He kissed the top of her head again. "I love you, kiddo. I don't know what I'd do if I lost you."

"Love you, too."

They sat like that a while. With the sound of birds and the distant drone of the mower, Jessie could have easily dozed off, but she forced herself to stay awake. It would be better to get back on a normal sleep schedule.

"Oh," James voice filled the long silence that had fallen. "I finished up the sale of the condo this morning. The proceeds should be in your bank account."

"Thanks, I really appreciate it." Might as well tackle the other beast while she was at it and sat up to look at him. "By the way, I'm planning to work a bit after I'm settled in, and before you say no, please I need to do something. I was already getting stir crazy in the hotel. And my therapist is encouraging me to try to get back to normal as much as I can. She thinks it will help with the nerves and fear, so that means working. I know Jack has some stuff I can do. Nothing heavy, and no outside clients yet, just internals and our trusted associates."

"Okay, okay, I won't argue. Just don't push yourself too hard." He ruffled her hair, like he used to when she was a kid. "Though I would think you'd have plenty to do dealing with this house. I mean she is a grand old girl, but she is showing her age pretty bad. We couldn't do much with it since Henry was too sick by then to deal with a bunch of reno noises, and before that, well, it's so easy to not realize your house is be-coming outdated until it suddenly smacks you in the head."

"Yeah, I know. I don't think it's in horrible shape, but the porch needs some shoring up, the floors need refinishing, most of the rooms need painting, I think the siding may need some work, and the electric and plumbing systems could use an overhaul. The kitchen is way too small and the appliances are decades old, and I'd like to update the bathrooms, too."

"Well, you know we'll help as much as we can, but none of us are talented in making home repairs. Some will require hiring professionals to tackle." James paused. "Though if you want, you can always move back to the family house while the work is done and leave it to me to oversee the work here."

She smiled at him, appreciating the gesture, but shook her head no. "Don't tempt me to take the easy way out. Hav-ing a bunch of strangers out here terrifies me, and I'll have to start small, but I was thinking about it on the drive down. I think I need to do this, I need to see if I can do it for myself and for Grandpa."

"Well, at least here you don't have to worry about all of the workers being total strangers. You'll probably know a lot of them, either from when you were a kid or before you moved, so hopefully, that helps. Speaking of, your neighbor over there, Galen, is a contractor and a very good renovator. He's done some nice work here in town, including remodel-ing the library. You'll love it when you're up for visiting. I think he might be a good choice to work with. He's a good guy, got a great little boy, and you can trust him."

Jessie agreed it probably would be easier to work with someone she knew and had vetted. A lingering voice reminded her she'd also vetted the monster that nearly killed her, but she shoved the thought aside. That was a failing on many levels, including wrongly trusting him just because of his job.

"I'll consider it, presuming he'd still be willing to work with me after this morning."

"I heard about that from Julian," James said with a laugh. "Don't worry, I'm sure he'll understand. A girl can't be too careful and, well, just let him know you're not really a morning person."

"Hey!" She exclaimed in mock outrage before joining him in laughter. Hopefully, she could make amends with Galen to have him consider the project and he'd be okay with having a coward for a client.

Chapter 6

THE BRIGHT AND WARM Saturday afternoon left enough chill in the air that Michael wore his jacket as he walked back from Derek's house. They had been friends since shortly after Michael and his father moved to town a few years ago, and they often hung out on weekend afternoons after finishing chores. Most of the time, they had fun together. Derek had his own TV and several video game systems they could play, which was awesome since Michael's dad said he wasn't old enough to have a system yet.

Today's game hadn't been quite as fun though. It wasn't the kind of games they usually played; Derek had borrowed one of his older brother's games. It had a lot of blood and cursing and people killing people for no reason. If Michael's dad found out about it, he knew he would be in for an earful and a half, and his dad might even stop letting him go play at Derek's again. Still, his dad had made it clear keeping secrets was no different from lying and lying was way worse than playing a game he shouldn't have. Whether to confess or just hope his dad never found out ran through his mind.

Kipper, seemingly oblivious to his young master's dilemma, trotted along beside him, his tail waving in the air and his pointed ears standing up straight as he looked side-to-side. Though Kipper had walked the same route many times before, he never seemed to get bored with it. They passed the familiar white fence before they reached home when Kipper started to strain at the leash.

Shaken from his thoughts, Michael corrected the puppy with a sharp pull of the leash. "No. That's Miss. Bradshaw's place now and Dad says we can't go there. What has you so excited anyway, it's just a field." Then he spotted the rabbit watching them from a few yards away. He considered moving across the street a little early, even though it meant walking with his back to traffic. Of course, that was also against the rules, but he wasn't sure which one he was supposed to follow, considering his dad had said to stay on their side of the road too.

Kipper gave the leash another tug. Michael's arm dropped to his side with the leash dangling free in his hand. The collar broke! Kipper's brown and black body took off running, gleefully chasing the petrified bunny towards Miss Bradshaw's property.

"Kipper! Get back here!" Michael ran after him, but the stubborn puppy and the rabbit moved at top speed, maneuvering easily over the uneven ground. Michael stumbled to keep up. "Kipper leave that rabbit alone! Come here right now, come here, I said!"

Tail wagging and a huge puppy grin on his face, Kipper ignored the boys calls and continued after the rabbit, chasing it over a small hill. He'd barely disappeared when Michael heard the puppy yelping in agony. Running as fast as he could, Michael crested the hill to find Kipper hopelessly trapped in a huge briar patch. Sharp thorns pierced him from all sides, causing his pain-filled cries.

"Hold on, boy, I'm coming. Just stay still." Michael tried to reach in to grab the puppy, but the thorns cut his hands so much he was forced out with his own pain-filled cries. Pleading with the puppy to stay still, Michael looked around for a stick to push the branches with when a deep bark startled him. Turning slowly, he found the most enormous dog he'd ever seen standing there, staring at him.

His dad had said the dog was mean, but it wasn't growling or snarling, just staring at him with its head tilted to the side. It was a beautiful dog, with long, thick cream-colored fur and bands of gray around its neck. More gray ran along the top of its thick, plumy tail, while its mouth and the tips of its pricked ears were solid black. Its shape reminded him of a sheepdog, only much larger.

"Um…hi. Nice doggie. Are you Miss Bradshaw's dog? My dad said you were huge, and oh boy, are you ever." Though scared, Michael tried to keep his voice calm. In school, they had been taught when dealing with strange dogs, it was important not to make them feel threatened, not that he thought much would scare a dog that size. The dog could easily eat him and Kipper in just a few bites.

"I'm really sorry I'm on your land when I shouldn't be, but my dog Kipper is stuck in that bush there, see? I promise we'll leave as soon as I get him out, so please don't hurt us." As Michael spoke, it tilted its head to the other side, looking for all the world like it was carefully listening to what he said.

The dog barked again before turning and running back towards the house. Breathing a sigh of relief, Michael turned and continued his search for a good stick to use. Finally finding one that looked sturdy enough, he shoved it into the briar patch and pushed against the first branch in his way. But the stick broke, sending the branch snapping back into Kipper, who renewed screaming in fresh agony. While Michael tried not to cry over just any little thing, his buddy's painful howls were too much and had tears flowing down his cheeks.

"I'm sorry, boy, I'm sorry. Just hang on, I'll get you out, I promise."

"What on earth is going on here?" The woman's voice made him jump out of his skin. He saw the dog again before seeing the woman now following it. She picked up her pace and moved past him towards the bush.

"He chased a rabbit and got stuck in there. We didn't mean to trespass, honest we didn't." Tears fell from Michael's chin and dropped down his neck. His stomach turned around and around inside.

The woman, presumably Miss Bradshaw, kept her back to him while securing her hair in a ponytail. "Take a deep breath and calm down. You won't help him by being upset yourself, it will only make him more afraid. He isn't too far in, which is good, stay back there so you don't get hurt."

Her voice was steady and calm and seemed more matter of fact than angry. Michael forced himself to take several deep breaths while he watched her work on freeing Kipper.

Chapter 7

JESSIE SPENT THE EARLY afternoon working in the back garden area, cleaning up the beds nestling against the house's wrap-around porch. She'd been at it for about an hour when Causy ran towards her barking. After sliding to a stop a few yards away, Causy barked twice more before turning and running back the other direction. In the distance, she could hear something crying out in pain. Without hesitation, Jessie dropped her tools and ran after her.

As Jessie assessed the situation, she was glad she wore a long-sleeved shirt and garden gloves. The yowling puppy had gotten itself buried deep inside the thorn bush, and she hoped she wouldn't have to go back to the house to get her shears to cut away the branches. Working methodically, she pulled at different branches to push them out of the way, hooking them on other stronger branches to keep them from snapping back. Inch-by-inch, she made her way towards the puppy, ignoring pinpricks in her knees as fallen burrs and thorns pushed through her jeans.

When she was close enough to reach the puppy, she pushed the last of the branches back with one hand, then grabbed the pup by the scruff of its neck. With a quick apology, she yanked it backward out of the bush. Continuing to hold the little dog by the scruff, she eased her other hand into place to help support some of its weight.

The crying boy started towards them, but Jessie shook her head. "Stay back. He still has thorns and burrs in his fur. If you touch him now, it will cause him more pain, and you might get hurt yourself. We need to pull these out carefully and treat his wounds." Spotting the blood of the boy's hands, she added, "As well as yours. Come with me."

Taking for granted the child would obey, she headed back to the house. The puppy's cries quieted to occasional whimpers. She carefully held him in a way as to avoid burying any of the thorns deeper. To Jessie's surprise, she wasn't bothered by the boy's presence. Perhaps because he was such a young child, the automatic fear hadn't triggered, at least not yet.

After retrieving a pair of tweezers and some antiseptic, she led the way into the kitchen. She showed the boy how to hold the puppy, then carefully removed the burrs and thorns from the poor dog. It withstood the treatment quietly, whining only when Jessie dealt with the last ones stuck in its paw pads. She spoke in a low comforting tone as she worked, hoping to ease the anxieties of both puppy and owner. With the last one removed, she gave the puppy a good petting, telling him how brave he was, and then set him on the floor with a small handful of dog biscuits.

Moving her chair closer to the boy, she gave him what she hoped was a reassuring smile. "Now it's your turn, can you be as brave as he was?"

The boy took a deep breath, as if gathering up all his courage, and nodded before holding out both hands. Fortunately, most of the thorns and burrs were in his clothes and hadn't broken the skin, but she still removed them as gently as possible. The boy winced slightly when she applied antiseptic to the scratches on his hands, but otherwise withstood the stings like a champion.

While she worked, Michael watched her curiously. He decided Miss Bradshaw was just as beautiful as Mr. Clark described. With her long wavy black hair and beautiful skin, her smile was kind. She had sounded a little abrupt at first, but her voice was as gentle as her treatment of his wounds.

He found it difficult not to stare at the strange glasses she wore. On one side, they were perfectly normal, and he could see her beautiful gray eye. He'd never seen anyone with gray eyes before, but now that he had, he decided it was now his favorite eye color.

The left side of her glasses, though, were very odd: the lens was solid black with a white cross painted on it. It made it impossible to see her eye, though the skin around it looked rough, like a scar.

Reminding himself that staring was rude, he realized he was being even ruder. "I'm sorry, Miss Bradshaw. I'm showing really bad manners today. I'm sitting here while you fix my hand and you helped Kipper too and I haven't even said thank you yet! Thank you, thank you so much, Miss Bradshaw."

"Well, you've said thank you now, so no worries." A hint of a smile touched her lips. "So, his name is Kipper, you can call me Jessie, but what should I call you?"

"Oh, sorry, I'm Michael. We're your neighbors across the street and down a ways."

"I see, so you're Galen's son?"

"Yes, ma'am." He wondered if she was still mad at his dad from the other day, but she didn't seem angry or bothered by his being there so maybe his dad had just misunderstood everything.

"You should probably give him a call and let him know where you are. If you were on your way home before Kipper's accident, I'd imagine you're probably late by now?"

Michael glanced at the clock in the kitchen. "You're right, I'm way late. Can I borrow your phone?"

"Of course, it's over here." She led them towards the front door where the house phone sat. Though almost everyone owned cell phones these days, he knew a lot of people in Cascade Falls also still used household phones too, so he wasn't surprised to see it. He quickly dialed his dad's cell number and let him know where he was. When he finished, he let Miss Bradshaw know his dad was on his way. His dad had been worried because he'd called to let Michael know he was running late and hadn't gotten an answer.

"Well, while we wait would you like something to drink? I have milk, orange juice, and water?"

"Milk sounds good."

Back in the kitchen, Jessie fixed them both tall glasses of milk and set them out at the table along with a platter of chocolate chip cookies she'd made earlier. "If your dad won't mind, you're welcome to have some of these too."

"Well, I'm usually allowed to have one or two around this time of day. I think he'll be fine with it."

As they sat together and enjoyed cookies, Michael caught himself staring at her face again. He knew he was being rude, but he couldn't help being curious as well. Trying to distract himself from acting so badly, he instead stared at her dog.

"I've never seen a dog that big ever. She's way bigger than the town's police dogs. She's a beautiful color though. What kind of dog is she?"

"She's a Caucasian Owtcharka and her name is Causy."

Michael's mouth dropped open. He wouldn't be able to pronounce that name in a million years. "She's a what again?"

Jessie laughed and repeated the name. "It is a mouthful, isn't it? Some people just call them Caucasian Mountain

Dogs. They are named for the Russian mountains where they came from."

"Oh, cool. How big is she anyway?"

"She's just over two feet tall at her shoulders, and she weighs about 140 pounds."

Michael's mouth fell open again. "One hundred and forty! Seriously? That's almost twice what I weigh! Whoa, you could flatten me, girl." The dog wagged her tail and came over when the boy spoke. To his delight, she let him pet her, solemnly waving her tail and smiling. "You're not a mean dog at all, are you? You're a nice girl. Your fur is so soft. Thank you for getting us help, we really appreciate it."

Jessie was surprised Causy had come over to the boy. A naturally reserved breed, she typically paid little attention to strangers beyond evaluating their potential threat. If someone other than Jessie attempted to pet her, she would turn her head away or move out of reach, but she seemed to have no problem letting this adorable towheaded boy stroke her fur and fondle her ears.

As they ate their second cookies, Jessie could tell Michael still wanted to ask about her glasses and her eye. Deciding to get it over with, she softly told him, "You can ask if you want."

If anything, he looked even more uncomfortable. "I'm sorry. I know I'm staring. My dad said it's really rude and it's rude to ask people about personal things like their appearance and stuff."

Wanting to help ease the boy's discomfort, Jessie's normal reticence about her appearance faded. "Well, I suppose that is true, but I figure we're sitting here sharing food and having gone through an emergency together, so that means we're becoming friends. When you're making friends, it's normal to want to know more about each other."

He smiled at that. "Yeah, I'd like to be friends. Mr. Clark talked about you all the time, he really loved you. So, it feels kind of like I know you already."

"I really loved him too. And I seem to remember him mentioning a friendly neighborhood boy who came to visit sometimes, so I guess we aren't strangers at all, are we?" she said with a smile, then took a deep breath as she tried to figure out how to word things for a boy his age. "As for my glasses, they are like this because my left eye doesn't work anymore. A bad man hurt it and now it looks very ugly. People don't like seeing it, so I wear these to cover it up."

Instead of teasing or being disgusted, Michael nodded solemnly. "Does it still hurt?"

"Sometimes, yes, but not as much anymore."

"I'm sorry about your eye. I think your glasses are kinda cool though."

With a smile, she thanked him, seeing the sincerity of his compliment in his earnest face. "How about another cookie?" He grinned back as he took the extended cookie and the conversation turned to dogs. Jessie suggested Kipper was in serious need of training and that he might want to ask his dad to let him enroll the pup in a beginning training course. "With proper training, you wouldn't have to worry as much about him running off and he would come back when called instead of ignoring you. It can also be fun. If he's good, there are competitions to see which dogs obey commands the best. Meanwhile, why don't I show you how to teach him to sit?"

She also told him how to pick a better collar for Kipper and gave him one of the slip leads she kept on hand to help him keep control of the pup until his collar could be replaced. They were still practicing the sitting when Galen arrived.

As he walked with Jessie to the front door, Michael realized her hand started to shake, and her face seemed lighter than before. He wanted to ask if she was okay but wasn't sure if it would be rude to point it out. He remembered seeing someone with shaky hands at the store once, and his dad had explained the man had a medical condition that made his hands do that. Somehow, though, he didn't think Jessie was sick. She seemed fine the whole time, but now as she opened the front door for him, he could tell something wasn't right.

Worried, he looked up at her, but she didn't say anything. He headed out to meet his dad at the top of the steps, but Jessie stayed inside behind the door, leaving the screen partly open. Michael looked back and remembered what she said about people not liking her eye. Maybe that's why she hid; she was worried his dad would stare or say something rude. He wanted to tell her not to worry, but his dad was already talking to her.

"Um, thanks for helping Michael and Kipper out. We really appreciate it. I hope he wasn't too much trouble," his dad said.

"No, it's…it's okay, they weren't any trouble. He's…he's a very nice boy." As Michael wondered why she spoke so stilted and sounded so scared, Galen thanked her again and headed back towards the car. His hand on Michael's back prompted him along with Kipper in tow.

Chapter 8

FROM THE MOMENT THEY climbed in the truck, Michael talked non-stop about Jessie and how "awesome" she'd been in saving Kipper and helping them. "And she is super smart about dogs. Look, she showed me how to get Kipper to sit!"

As they entered the kitchen, Michael demonstrated by grabbing a piece of dog food and standing in front of Kipper. He put his hand in a fist around the treat. "Sit." He moved the treat low and over the pup's head until Kipper's butt hit the ground, then Michael praised him and gave him the food.

"See? Isn't that cool! She said if I do it every day, he'll pick it up real quick! Oh, and to make sure to do it without food sometimes too, so he doesn't only do it for food. Oh, and she gave us this cool leash. She said it's called a slip lead because it slips over his head, like this."

Galen was amused at his son's obvious infatuation with the woman. Galen himself had barely seen her hidden behind the screen. Still, he didn't think it would be good to encourage Michael to get too attached to their new neighbor. He was grateful she'd helped his son and wayward puppy, but he couldn't forget she had sent her dog after them. If it had it just been him, he could explain the behavior as her being used to living in the city and being cautious of strangers, but Phillip had been in uniform.

Besides, what kind of person had she grown into if she hadn't even come to see her supposedly "beloved grandfather" in the entire last month he'd spent in the hospital before he'd died? Surely if she was any kind of decent person, she'd have made time for him in her busy life to at least say goodbye. Such a woman who seemed to have little regard for people she was supposed to be close to didn't seem like someone who would make a good role model for Michael.

He turned to say something to that effect when Michael started talking again. "Jessie's dog is so cool! Oh, her name is Causy by the way. She is a cacas…causca…um, a big Russian mountain dog. I can't remember how to pronounce the real word. Anyway, did you know she weighs twice as much as me! Talk about huge! And she's really smart too, knows lots of commands!"

"Really?" Galen lifted his eyebrow with skepticism as he motioned for Michael to sit at the kitchen table.

"Yep, Jessie said she won a bunch of obedience awards. Oh, and if I work hard with Kipper, he could try to win awards too! That would be awesome, wouldn't it?"

"It would certainly be awesome if he obeyed you instead of running off." Galen said with a smile. "But, you know her dog can be rather unfriendly too, and he came after your uncle and me. I'm not sure—"

Before he could finish, Michael shook his head. "She's just 'reserved' around strangers, that's all. Um, dad, did you, did you bully Jessie when you were kids or something?"

Taken aback, Galen stared open-mouthed at his son for a moment. Surely Jessie wasn't telling his son lies about him. "Did she say something like that?"

"Oh no, she didn't. It's just, she seemed kind of scared when you came to pick me up, so I wondered why. Though I guess that would be a long time to be scared of you if that was it…anyway, that's probably why Causy came after you. She's protective of Jessie and she probably knew Jessie was scared."

While relieved Jessie hadn't lied, he was bothered to think she feared him, much less letting his son think that. He could maybe understand caution, if she didn't remember him, but outright fear. "How did she seem scared?"

Michael opened and closed his mouth, then shrugged. "Just a guess. Maybe she was just tired."

Galen decided to drop the conversation for now. Michael's sudden interested in the table in front of him and the obvious shuffling of feet under said table made him suspect Michael might have decided he said something he shouldn't have.

"Okay. Well, I'm glad things had turned out okay and she was helpful to you both. Still, I'd rather you not go over there again for now, okay? I don't trust that dog and while Miss Bradshaw was nice today, she's probably busy and wouldn't want you dropping in all the time."

"But dad, she said we were becoming friends. Shouldn't friends visit each other?"

"That's true, but remember how we talked about friends you can visit at home and those you can't?"

"Yeah, I can only go to a friend's house once you've met their parents and feel comfortable with them." He paused and furrowed his brow. "I guess since Jessie is an adult, you'd have to meet her and get to know her before I can visit?"

"Exactly. While we knew each other as kids, that was a long time ago, so it's kind of like we're strangers again. Okay?"

"Okay. Though I hope you get to know each other soon because I really had fun visiting with her."

Disappointed, Michael led Kipper up to his room and he sat on the edge of his bed.

Absently petting the dog's head, he wondered again about why Jessie was scared of his dad and about why someone would hurt her like that and why his dad didn't seem to like her. He'd avoided explaining about her acting scared, since he thought it might be gossiping and his dad had said that was bad.

He could sort of understand about the stranger thing, but he also suspected his dad wasn't going to go over and make friends anytime soon. He really liked Jessie and wanted to talk to her about dog training and stuff. She talked to him like he was an adult, not like a dumb kid as some adults did.

He wanted to talk to someone about everything that had happened. With the way his dad was acting about Jessie though, it didn't feel like they could have a good talk about it. Besides, if he did talk his dad, maybe he'd accidentally say something she wouldn't want to be shared or would make his dad dislike her even more. Looking at the picture of his mom on his dresser, Michael realized there was someone he could talk to without worrying about gossiping or anything. Feeling better about having a plan, he went over to his desk to finish the rest of his weekend homework.

Chapter 9

FOR THE FOURTH TIME, Jessie reached for the handle to step out of the car. And for the fourth time, she drew her hand back again. Her phobia didn't affect her ability to drive a car. Knowing people didn't really look at each other's faces while driving was one of the only reasons she could make the drive from Chicago. Getting out of the car away from home, though, was still another matter.

Causy whined and nudged her shoulder, reminding her they still sat in the parking lot of the cemetery. Jessie peered around at the empty lot, hoping nobody else was walking throughout the grounds. It was a small cemetery and the middle of a Saturday afternoon. Her hand shook on the door handle as she tried to open it again.

She jumped and her heart raced as she realized someone was standing outside the door, staring at her. Before panic could overtake her completely, she recognized the young boy Michael whom she'd helped yesterday. He gave her a small wave, concern etched on his face. Taking a deep breath, she pushed the button to roll the window down.

"Hey Jessie, you okay?"

"Yeah," she lied while trying to keep her voice steady. "I wanted to visit Grandpa's grave, but I'm not actually sure where it is."

"Oh, I know where. Want me to show you? I'm going to walk past it anyway."

Cornered in her lie, Jessie forced herself to nod, put the window back up, and finally opened the door. Causy practically crowded her out, pushing enormous body against her side, as if trying to force her past the fear.

Michael smiled and held out his hand. "Come on, it's right this way."

She placed her hand in his little one. Could he feel her shaking? Jessie's head whipped left to right, assuring herself nobody else was in the parking lot and that nobody else would notice her trembling hands. If Michael noticed, he said nothing, and simply led her down the freshly mowed rows. Causy followed behind.

A third of the way into the cemetery, he turned and led her past a dozen graves until they stood in front of Grandpa's.

"Here you go." He smiled at her again. "I'll leave you two to talk. I'm visiting someone over that way." He thumbed to the right. "See you later."

She managed to whisper a thank you before the little boy moved on his way, leaving her and Causy standing in front of her grandfather's grave. She watched the boy continue further back into the graveyard until barely visible in the opposite corner. Remembering Galen was a widower, she wondered if the person Michael visited was his mother.

Grandpa's grave was marked with a simple, but elegant stone, with his name, date of birth, date of death, and an epitaph listing him as a beloved friend and grandfather. Seeing the word on his grave broke free the grief inside her. With a sob, she fell to her knees in front of the grave.

Michael continued to his mother's grave. Why did Jessie sit in her car for a long time? He'd watched her doing so for a few minutes before deciding to approach her. His mom's grave was near the back of the cemetery at a pretty little spot with a nice thick tree shading it. Though she had died in Cary, where they used to live, his father had her moved to Cascade Falls so they could visit her whenever they wanted. He thought his mom would approve, as she had spoken fondly of the town and it seemed a peaceful place to rest.

Sitting on the ground in front of her grave, he told her all about his dad and Jessie. When he was done, he prayed and asked his mom to help him do the right thing, to help his dad see Jessie's nice nature, and to help them be friends. He sat a while longer, updating his mom about school and his friends, before finally telling her thanks for listening and getting up to leave.

On his way back, from a few rows down, he spotted Jessie still sitting on her knees in front of Mr. Clark's grave, her face buried in her hands. Causy sat behind with her head on her master's shoulder. Jessie cried hard, and it hurt him to listen. He thought she must be grieving badly to cry like that, it reminded him of how much he had cried when his mom died.

He couldn't stand watching her, so he quietly called her name and joined her. Though he was pretty sure she heard him, she didn't answer. Michael walked closer and wrapped his arms around her, hugging her tight while she continued crying. After a while, her sobs quieted, and she lifted her head to look at him a moment before lowering it again.

"Oh, Michael, I'm sorry. I must seem like a pretty pathetic adult to be sitting here crying like this." Michael lowered himself to the ground next to her and held her hand.

"I don't think so. You must have really loved Mr. Clark a lot is all. My dad loved my mom lots too, and he cried like that after she died." He handed her the handkerchief from his back pocket so she could wipe her face. As she did, he realized her bad eye hadn't made any tears. That seemed kind of sad to him, but for now, he was glad she'd stopped crying.

After she finished drying her face, she looked over at Mr. Clark's grave while she spoke softly. "I did love him. He was the only grandpa I ever knew. My own grandparents all died before I was born. When I was a teenager, he was never too busy or too tired to chat and he always knew the most interesting things. He taught me about stars and flowers and how to track wildlife. Some folks thought I was weird for spending time with him, but I didn't care. I thought he was cool. Even after I moved to Chicago, we talked regularly by phone and by letters. He didn't like email or computers. Said it meant more to put pen to paper, so he'd write me and I'd write back."

Tears started streaming from her good eye again. "He loved me so much too, and I couldn't even be here for him when he needed me most. God I wish I'd known how sick he was so I could have come home months ago. I should have been here with him when he was dying." Her voice broke as she continued, "I know he asked for me over and over, but because I was stupid and trusted the wrong person, I didn't get to say goodbye."

Michael hugged her again as she started crying, though not as bad as before. He tried to imagine what it would have been like to not have been able to say goodbye to his mom and he could understand why she was crying. When she quieted again, he couldn't stop himself from asking, "That person you trusted…is he the bad man who hurt your eye?"

She nodded. "Yes, that was him. When grandpa died, I was still in the hospital recovering. My family didn't tell me at first, not wanting to upset me since they knew I couldn't be here. I didn't find out he died until a month ago. I decided to come out today and say goodbye and that I was sorry, but I wonder if he hears me?"

"Of course he does," Michael told her with absolute conviction. "I'm sure he's up in heaven now, glad to see you, and I bet he's happy to know you are living in his house. He loved you lots and lots, so I'm positive he understands. He's probably more worried about you than anything and hoping you'll be okay."

Through tears, Jessie couldn't help but choke out a small laugh. "You know, you're a pretty smart kid."

"Yep, that's what my dad says…though sometimes he adds another word I'm not allowed to say at the end."

Jessie laughed out loud while wiping away the last round of tears. "Well, I don't know about that, but I do thank you for coming over here and comforting me. It means a lot."

"That's what friends are for, right?" Looking over at his adorable smile, Jessie nodded with a smile of her own. He stood and held out his hand. "Hey, you want to meet my mom. She's over that way."

Touched, Jessie stood and took his hand, letting him lead the way. When they reached the grave of Melinda Andrews, Michael gravely introduced them. "Mom, this is my new friend Jessie I was telling you about. Jessie, this is my mom Melinda."

Matching his tone, Jessie greeted the grave. "I'm honored to meet you. You have the most wonderful son and I know you must be very proud of him."

As they started to leave, Michael let go of Jessie's hand to run back to his mom's grave. "I almost forgot. Mom, remember my friend Mr. Clark? He's Jessie's grandpa and he's up there with you so can you help him learn the ropes and stuff? Thanks."

Jessie nearly cried anew over the boy's innocent and touching request. When he returned to her side, he grabbed her hand and they left the cemetery together, walking back hand-in-hand until they reached her SUV, where they hugged then parted ways. Heading back to his house, Michael decided he probably shouldn't tell his dad about seeing Jessie. Technically he knew he would be lying, but this was definitely one of those private things not to be shared.

Chapter 10

JESSIE MADE SCANT PROGRESS on the renovation, in large part due to her inability to pick up the phone and call Galen. She'd already gone through the house room-by-room and sorted out what would be kept, sold, or given away, and what furnishings and decorations she wanted to add. She'd also made a list of the work that needed to be done as well as putting together a large notebook filled with clippings, sketches, work lists, and price estimates for everything.

The one thing she'd managed to avoid doing was looking up Galen's number. Every morning, she'd tell herself "this is the day," but by evening she'd "accidentally" overlook it until it was too late. Thanks to the Internet, she knew she'd be able to order furnishings, fixtures, and what-not and have it shipped directly to the house. Jazza brought her a veritable pile of paint samples from the local store for picking colors. Still, Jessie needed professionals for a lot of the work. As she crawled into bed her first Friday night in the house, she'd again pledged to look up Galen's number and call him.

She did at least manage to look up the number, but another week passed without her calling. Jessie had been home just over two weeks, and she kept finding something, anything, that just had to be done, keeping her from calling. The third time she picked up and put down her phone, even Causy groaned at her in seeming irritation.

"If it's so easy, you do it." she grumbled back at the dog, then picked up the phone again. Closing her eyes, she took deep breaths. It was only a phone call; he might not even be interested in taking the job. Unbidden, the memory of Michael comforting her at Grandpa's grave came to mind, and she found herself drawing a small boost of strength from that quiet show of support. She quickly dialed the number before she could chicken out again.

"Andrews Renovations. This is Galen." The deep voice filling her ear nearly made her send the phone flying. She hadn't even heard it ring.

"Hello?" This time, his voice held a touch of impatience.

"Um…hello, this is Jessie…Jessie Bradshaw." Silently she cursed herself for not controlling the fear that made her speak in such a hesitant way.

"Oh, hey. What can I do for you?"

"I…I want to do some work on the house, and, wondered if…if you might be interested in working on the project?" There, she did better that time, didn't she? Did it sound more normal?

"Sure, I'd love to talk to you about it. If you like, I can stop by around, say, 2:30 to go over the work you want done so I can get a quote worked up?"

Come over? Of course, of course, he must come over. Unable to stop herself from quivering, Jessie still managed to agree to the time and say goodbye before the fear could win. Dropping the phone on the green velour sofa beside her, she exhaled loudly. She'd done it! Causy came over and nuzzled Jessie as if to reward her for a job well done.

"I really did it, girl. He's coming over. Now, I just have to not freak out and make him think I'm an even more horrible weirdo than he probably already does."

As the time ticked closer to their agreed to time, she sat on her hands to keep from calling James and begging him to come handle the meeting with Galen. She knew all she had to do was tell him she was scared, and he'd drop everything to come over. Part of her desperately wanted to, while the part of her determined to heal knew she couldn't rely on her brother forever, nor did she want to end up being a burden on him. He'd given up much of his youth to raise her and be both father and brother. He didn't need a child to take care of again, unless it was his own.

Though she knew logically Galen was unlikely to want to harm her, or that Causy would let him, she trembled at the thought of being alone with him. She tried to remember the Galen she'd known as a teenager. He'd been a nice guy, polite, treated girls like people instead of objects, and hadn't been inclined to serial date like other teens. Indeed, as far as she knew, he'd remained faithful to his girlfriend back home during all his visits, despite having plenty of interest from the local girls. Now that she thought about it, had that girl been Melinda, Michael's late mom? Had he married his high school sweetheart, only to lose her far too young?

I can do this, I can do this, I can do this! She repeated the mantra over and over again as she waited. By the time Causy barked to announce to Galen's arrival, she'd almost convinced herself. Jessie raced to the window. As she watched his truck come up the drive, she wondered how he would react to her face. It wasn't personal vanity that made her acknowledge she'd been a beautiful woman before the attack; she'd been offered modeling jobs when she was younger, though they hadn't interested her at all. Now with her scarred-up face and overly thin body, she doubted Galen would even see her as a female. Surely, someone who raised such a sweet boy wouldn't be as bad as the people back in Chicago. If nothing else, she hoped Galen's Southern manners would keep him from commenting at all. Needing to do something with all her nervous energy, she grabbed the notebook with all her plans and went outside with Causy trotting at a perfect heel at her side.

With his metal storage clipboard in hand, Galen was half-way to the porch when Jessie came out wearing a simple, long sleeve blue blouse, jeans, and a white wide-brim hat. Seeing the huge dog, he took two steps back.

"It's okay…she isn't going to hurt you," Jessie said quickly, then looked at the dog, pointed at Galen, and said, "friend." The dog glanced at him before looking back at her and barked once. With a nod, Jessie started down the stairs toward him. He thought she hesitated a bit before going down them. She was unnaturally pale, and her hands were visibly trembling. She really was seriously afraid of him?

When she stopped a foot away, he forgot the question as he noticed the strange glasses she wore. *What on earth?* As he noticed the scar tissue around the edge of her covered eye, he realized while he'd been staring she still hadn't said anything. Kicking himself for his rudeness, he held out his hand and looked down dubiously at the staring dog. "Hey, that is one big dog. Michael mentioned something about her being a mountain breed?"

"Yes, she's a Caucasian Owtcharka. It's a herding breed originally developed in the Caucasian mountains near the Russian-Georgia border."

The pathetic attempt she made at a smile she while talking did little to erase the obvious discomfort on her face. She'd even managed to avoid shaking his hand without seeming to be rude, and he suspected if he hadn't been watching her carefully, he'd have not even noticed her leaving his outstretched hand untouched.

Hesitant to deal with someone with issues, Galen debated calling it off, but his instincts told him that would be the wrong thing to do. It wasn't that he had a pressing need for work; he received plenty of business both locally and from other towns around the county, and in some other counties as well thanks to Internet advertising. Regardless of how she seemed to feel about him, she was willing to work with him professionally. Besides, this was the Clark house, his dream project. He wouldn't turn down the chance to work on the house merely because she acted oddly.

So instead, he gestured toward the notebook and asked if she wanted to start outside. Her relief was palpable as she agreed. Jessie walked over to the left side of the porch to look at the cedar siding. "I thought of painting the whole outside…there is an old picture of the house when it was, um, first built and it was a light blue color. I think…I think I'd like to have it back that color."

"Yeah, I must admit, this salmon is really not doing the house any favors," Galen said with a chuckle as he started taking notes on the legal pad clipped to the outside of the clipboard. He prodded some of the shingles and made some more notes. "At first glance, I'd say the outside isn't in bad shape physically, but some of these pieces need replacing, especially at the bottom, and we'll need to check for any signs of rot or damage. They can be tricky to replace, but this style is easy enough to match."

"Yes…I thought that might be the case." She held her notebook so tightly, her knuckles were white, but still, she looked up. "I also want to replace all the windows. Most can be in the same places, I think, but some rooms I want to redo the whole layout, including the windows. For those…those that stay in place, I want double-pane glass for better energy efficiency."

"Good idea, they can save a ton on heating and cooling costs, and they come in a lot of styles, so we can still match the original feel of the house while taking advantage of modern improvements." They walked around to the back of the house. Galen paused now and then to check something on the wall, porch, or to inspect the foundation. As they talked, Jessie spoke in halts, with the occasional repeated or stuttered word, but she seemed to grow more confident the longer they went on. And so far, he approved of her ideas for the house; they seemed well suited to modernizing the house while retaining its historical feel and uniqueness.

Before heading inside, they discussed the roof. Without climbing up, Galen was pretty sure it would need replacing soon as it looked well past its prime and some of the fascia obviously rotten.

"That's actually good, I think. I…I'd kind of like to look at putting in solar shingles instead of regular ones. That way the roof will look normal and there won't have to be big solar panels on it, but it'll be a nice energy improvement."

Galen thought a moment. "Now, I haven't worked with them personally, but I have an associate over in Asheville who has, so I'll need to talk with him on the details there, but I like the idea. It seems a pretty good way to make a house much more environmentally friendly while doing work that already needs to be done."

Jessie led the way inside, her grip moving from the notebook to the dog's fur. Galen was surprised the dog wasn't whining from how tightly Jessie's fist clenched. As they passed through the small mudroom leading into the kitchen, Galen watched silently as she took several deep breaths. Seemingly calmer, she moved into the kitchen, removing her hat and hanging it on a chair at the kitchen table.

"I...I was thinking of getting rid of the mudroom there and stealing that space for the kitchen. This is one room that really must be modernized. I want to completely redo the whole thing. It is too small, there isn't enough counter space, and the appliances are all old."

Galen had to agree. The L-shaped counters only held a microwave and coffee maker, but already seemed cluttered. "So, I'm guessing you want to blend style and function? Do you like to cook a lot?"

"Yes...and I love to bake. I can't bake much in that small oven other than cookies and brownies."

"Do you want to keep this an eat-in kitchen?"

"No...not if it's possible." This time her hesitancy seemed to come more from uncertainty than the unnamed fear. She pointed to the wall in front of them where a door led off somewhere. "That next room is a formal dining room. I'd really love to take down the wall, so the rooms flow together, and then on that side, have a breakfast bar, maybe with a built-in cooktop?"

"I'd need to check to see if it's load-bearing, but we should be able to do something either way. If it's load-bearing, we'd have to add in support, but otherwise, it can still work. Do you have any ideas about materials?"

"Oh, yes." She set the notebook on the battered old table taking up half the kitchen space and flipped it open. Inside, Galen saw tabbed sections for each room and appreciated her organization. In the kitchen section, she showed him the face-framed maple cabinets she wanted, and he agreed the style would work well for bringing in some of the house's original feel. For the counters, she'd continued her theme of trying to be environmentally friendly by selecting recycled glass counters and flooring, in different patterns of blues and whites.

"Those are nice color choices. I like how you went with a smaller gradient for the counters, but a larger, more dramatic one in the floors." Spotting the next page, he noticed she'd picked all energy efficient appliances, with custom blue finishes to complement the counters. "I think, with your plans here, we can make you a gorgeous kitchen. I should probably ask what kind of budget we're looking at?"

"Um…well, I hadn't really thought about it, but my condo sold for $750,000. Since Grandpa left the house to me, all I had to pay was taxes and utilities, so most of it is still left. I think $700,000 would be enough, do you?"

"I'd, uh, I'd say that should be plenty, depending on what else you have in mind. Guess we'd better see the rest." Galen tried wrapping his head around the figure as they moved through the rest of the downstairs. She'd said it so casually, almost like an afterthought. He knew the Bradshaws were extremely wealthy, heck everyone did, but still he hadn't really thought about how it would apply with Jessie and the project. With that kind of budget, they could do a lot with the house. Still, when he finished the quote, he'd make sure they also discussed what kind of value the renovations would add to the house, so Jessie could be well-informed about any potential return on her investment.

The rest of the downstairs consisted of a large, airy living room in the front of the house separated from the dining room by a modest foyer, the stairs to the second floor with a guest bathroom under them, and a guest bedroom in the back used as a home office. Most of the rooms only needed general work: some painting, window replacements, and restoring the crown molding, baseboards, and the badly damaged hardwood floors. Galen was confident they could be restored rather than having to replace them, which seemed to make her happy. In the living room, she wanted to refinish the fireplace and install a wall-mounted flat-panel TV and sound system. She wanted to add built-in bookcases in the office, so it could double as a home library, and do a complete remodel of the guest bathroom, which looked like something out of the 50s. Jessie mentioned upgrading all the wiring and the plumbing, as needed, to bring things up to code to better support all the new appliances and electronics.

As they headed upstairs, she released her grip on the dog and seemed at least a little more at ease with him. He'd been careful to speak in lower, calmer tones, to avoid adding to her anxiety. On the second floor, the stairs turned, and the rooms were oriented perpendicular to the bottom floor, the master bedroom and attached bath took up the back half of the house. Two guest bedrooms shared another bathroom, occupying the front. The guest rooms were primarily paint jobs, but both bathrooms needed complete overhauls. In the master, she blushed as she showed him a pricey overflow tub with a ceiling mounted pour spout she'd picked out.

"I…I know it's an indulgence, but I've wanted one of those since I first saw them a few years ago. Do you…do you think we could make it work?"

"The plumbing won't be a major problem, just have to run new pipes, but space is an issue. With the tub, the separate shower, and putting in larger master closets, things will be tight. We could steal room from the other bedrooms, but then they'd lose size as well." He paused a moment, solutions quickly running through his head. "Another possible option, since this takes up the back of the house anyway, would be to expand the bathroom out over the porch. We could get enough room for the additions, and still maintain the outdoor balcony off your bedroom."

"Oh, that sounds perfect."

They headed downstairs, discussing lighting options for the various rooms. Galen also noted they'd need inspections of the heating and air conditioning systems, since they would need modifications for the room rearrangements. At the front door, Galen let her know it would take a while to put together a quote and proposed work packet, but he'd touch base with her at the end of the week in either case.

"Alright, sounds good. Thank you for coming and I look forward to hearing from you." Galen decided the smile she gave him, while shaky, was genuine. She still managed not to shake his outreached hand before he turned and headed back to his truck. Driving back to his office, he caught himself humming as he contemplated the project and what he hoped was progress in getting Jessie to like him again.

Chapter 11

AFTER CLOSING THE FRONT door, Jessie fell back against it and slid to the ground. With a worried whine, Causy nuzzled her.

"I'm okay, girl, I'm okay. I just can't believe it. I got through it, all of it." Checking her watch, she realized they had talked for nearly two hours. While the irrational fears had kept a hold of her the whole time, she'd managed to keep it under control, and by the end she'd almost been able to talk and act relatively normal. Her psychologist would no doubt say it was a big achievement when she reported in for their monthly appointment, and she wasn't about to let the thought of the hordes of strangers coming through the house to do the actual work ruin her bit of joy. "You know girl, I feel like celebrating a little."

After checking to see what ingredients she had on hand, she called Jazza to invite her to dinner. When she arrived, Jazza brought with her a bottle of wine and a sinful looking strawberry-topped cake. They shared a hug at the door before moving to the kitchen. While Jessie pulled the chicken out of the oven and quickly made a pan-gravy with some of its drippings, Jazza served the wine and set the table. Over the meal of herb roasted chicken, homemade mashed potatoes and gravy, and tossed salad, Jessie told her about calling Galen and his subsequent trip to the house.

"Good for you! I'd call that a big step forward, and a welcome one. I know this all must be frustrating for you, being so afraid of going out. I hate there isn't more I can do to help."

"Thank you, and I know you and my brothers would do anything for me. This is, unfortunately, one battle I have to tackle as much as I can on my own. Knowing you all are supporting me helps more than you realize though," Jessie told her truthfully, then decided to change the subject, not wanting to ruin her good mood by getting too much into her issues. "Speaking of steps forward, I don't see any new rings. Is my brother still being a mule?"

"Are you kidding? If you look in the dictionary under mule, you'll find his picture," Jazza said with a laugh, but her smile fell away quickly. "You know, it wouldn't be so frustrating if he'd at least tell me why he won't marry me, it's the not knowing that's as aggravating as anything."

Jessie didn't understand why James was balking either. She and Jazza had been best friends since she was seven and Jazza ten. Jazza had been in love with Jessie's oldest brother for nearly as long. Of course, at first, he'd only seen Jazza as the friend of his kid sister and had kindly deflected the young girl's crush without hurting her feelings. But then at twenty-one, Jazza had let him know in no uncertain terms exactly how she felt and what she wanted from him, regardless of his being twelve years her senior.

Jessie and her siblings had taken something of a perverse delight in watching her brother squirm due to the age difference and his conflicting feelings on having partially raised her alongside Jessie after the death of her parents with their mom. But in the end, Jazza had gotten him to put aside the image of the little girl he'd known and see the young woman in front of him, and he'd fallen like a ton of bricks for the vivacious, gentle-hearted girl. They'd been together ever since, and no one doubted his love for Jazza, but even after all this time, he wouldn't marry her, nor would he live with her.

"Well, you know me, I won't give up. I'll wear him down eventually, I'm sure of it. So tell me, is Mr. Andrews as gorgeous as he was as a teenager?" At Jessie's raised eyebrow, Jazza laughed. "Hey, I love your brother, but it doesn't mean my eyes stopped working."

Laughing, Jessie tried to evaluate Galen as neutrally as she could before answering. "I guess you could say that. He still has that thick brown hair and those chocolate-colored eyes. I'd say he has filled out nicely, all that working on houses has made him muscular, but not big and bulky. And he has a nice voice. Calm and soothing."

"Now that's the Jess I know. So, you like him?"

"Before, I'd have probably said yes without a moment's hesitation. Now…now, I would say he is a nice guy and certainly easy on the eyes, but I couldn't help being afraid. I shook half the time and held onto poor Causy's fur to make it through."

"Hmm, but you did eventually let her go, right?"

"You…you're right, I did. When he left, I hadn't been holding her for a while."

Jazza smiled at her and patted her hand. "Well, there ya go. It's all baby steps, hon, and that you actually noticed he's a hunky male is a darn good baby step to take."

"Hey, I never said hunky!" Jessie laughed, but privately she agreed with the basic assessment.

Over thick slices of rich cake, they chatted about Jessie's plans for the house, as well as Jazza's plans to expand her restaurant, Razzmatazz. She'd opened it after graduating college as a place for locals and any passers-through to enjoy authentic home-style cuisine, all prepared from family recipes submitted by locals. To pay proper homage to the contributors, each dish was named after the family or person who wrote it.

With Jessie's love of cooking, it was no surprise the menu featured Jess's Cheesy Macaroni, as well as Bradshaw French Toast. Offering a flair of flexibility, Jazza allowed almost anything on the menu to be mixed and matched and everything was available at all hours instead of having set breakfast, lunch, and dinner hours.

"So, I'm thinking I want to include more regional and international cuisine to help reflect our growing multicultural population."

"I think that's a terrific idea. Do you already have an idea of what dishes you want to add?"

"Yep, I have a bunch of possible recipes gathered up and ready to try. I'm thinking of doing a tasting party in early November, just us family and a few select guests. I'd really love it if you could be there. You have a great sense of taste, so I really want your opinion."

Jessie wanted to say no, but this was Jazza, her best friend and practically her sister. With it being mainly family, it sounded doable. If there were guests, the only ones she could think of would be the Aria sisters, who were also like family to them, and whoever Julian or Julianna might be dating, if it was serious enough for that. Jack didn't date anyone seriously enough to bring to family events, especially ones like this. Still, she could feel her insides tighten at the thought. "I'll try, I'll definitely try."

"Good. I know you can do it." Jazza said with a smile and another hug before heading home.

Chapter 12

IN THE MORNING, JESSIE decided it was time to take another step towards healing by getting back to work as she told James she planned to do. Theoretically, she could have stopped working for years and been fine financially, thanks to her investments. Even without them, James would take care of her, if she wanted. While he was never one to spoil his siblings, he'd also understand her reluctance to work again.

After all, it was through her work that man had found her and destroyed her life in the first place. In some ways, the thought of working again was almost as terrifying as trying to go to the store, but she was running out of putter projects around the house, and even once the renovations started, she would mostly just be approving things, which wouldn't fill up the long days ahead.

First things first, setting up a work space. The back room on the first floor was arguably a guest bedroom, but Grandpa had always used it as his home office back when he still worked as a teacher at the local high school. It had a large L-shaped mahogany desk dominating the room, one of the furniture pieces she planned to keep during the renovations, along with the ultra-comfortable matching chair. The room was otherwise empty, save for the couple of boxes Jessie put in the room when she first came home and the extra-large dog bed, thanks to Jazza making a run to the pet store for her.

"Okay, girl, time to rejoin the twenty-first century."

Two hours later, her desktop computer was set up on the desk alongside the laptop computer she'd set up shortly after moving in. A scanner, printer, fax system, and NAS system were installed in the built-in bookcases along the walls. The desktop and laptop ran through her special router and custom scrambling system before connecting to the high-speed modem while the NAS was isolated to her internal private network.

With everything ready, now came the hard part. Actually working. The familiar tremors started at the thought, but she forced herself to sit down and power up the desktop. With it offline so long, of course the first thing she saw after logging in was a notice about system updates. Using it as the perfect procrastination excuse, she left them to install while she found chores "needing" to be done. After a basket of laundry was loaded and a partial load of dishes started, she gave herself a mental kick at her pathetic avoidance efforts. With a deep breath, she headed to the kitchen and fixed herself a cup of coffee and picked up a cinnamon roll, the way she always used to start her work days. Coffee and a pastry. She hoped the routine would help as she headed back to the home office. Causy following patiently along.

Hand still shaking, she forced herself to call Jack to let him know she was ready to start working again and see if he had anything for her. Part of her hoped he'd say no, but he had six folks who'd come to the area in the last two weeks that needed checking. After getting the names and basics he had, she decided that at least starting with internal requests was easier, it was safe. She didn't have to fear her clients would harm her, that much was certain.

A highly skilled researcher, Jessie could find information on just about anyone or anything that could be found, be it places, topics, or people. For the family, she ran all the background checks on new people who wanted to live in Cascade Falls. Her brothers often joked her files were deeper than anything a CIA or FBI agent might have, and it was true. In addition to all the standard methods of gathering information, Jessie could, and regularly did, hack into various law enforcement and other private networks to gather data that might be hidden from more public systems.

Jack was usually in charge of monitoring who came to town, and then he would pass that info on to Jessie for the checks. Bad spots in their past didn't necessarily mean someone would be unwelcome. Indeed, for many, Cascade Falls was intended to be haven for those wanting to make a fresh start without their pasts shackling them down. As such, the town had a higher than average number of citizens with arrests and questionable activities in their pasts, and if they were so inclined, there were plenty of colorful stories to be heard.

Shaking off the fear, Jessie got to work on the internal requests. Browsing through databases, websites, records, and the like soothed her and kept her mind off things. The lingering unease soon faded, and she lost herself in her work as she often did before, pausing only to let Causy out for a midday walk and to throw together a quick sandwich for lunch. After lunch, she logged into her secure email account to see what requests had come in from private clients. Not quite ready to deal with instant spikes of fear that jolted through her at each request from a stranger, she declined everything but two simple requests from longtime clients she knew well enough to not be have a gut reaction against.

The sun had set when she finally stood, stretched, and locked both systems. Her growling stomach let her know dinner was running late. She frowned as she peered into the fridge, trying to will it to have more food than she saw. There wasn't much left from what James had brought when she first moved in. Shaking her head, she put the thought out of her mind for now and settled for heating up a can of soup. While feeding Causy, she realized the big dog's food container was also running low, only a few days' worths left at most.

There was no denying it, she needed groceries again. Biting her lip, she pondered the easy answer, calling James to have him do another delivery. But she didn't want to have to spend the rest of her life burdening her family like this. Deciding to take her successful meeting with Galen and her working again as good signs, she would try going to the store herself, first thing tomorrow.

Chapter 13

AFTER LEARNING GALEN HAD visited Jessie to discuss working on her house, Michael had questioned his dad nearly non-stop about the visit, what he thought of her, how she was doing, and if he now knew her well enough that Michael could visit again. Realizing his son wouldn't give up and forget his interest in their new neighbor, Galen relented and agreed to visits.

"However, you have to make sure it's okay with her. She might be busy or working, so you can't go over randomly without being sure it isn't a bother, understand?"

"Yep." Michael agreed with a nod, as he grinned ear to ear. He was practically dancing in place, no doubt ready to run over right then and there.

Though he had cautioned the boy about interrupting her work, Galen realized he didn't know what she did. Anytime he went past the house, her car was always there, in practically the same spot since she'd first arrived. Maybe she worked from home or was between jobs? She'd been there too long to be on an extended leave, unless her employer was ridiculously generous with their time off.

Then again, what exactly did any of the Bradshaws do for a living? As far as he knew, Julian was the only one with a regular job, though his twin Julianna's kennels seemed to be doing well enough that maybe she earned her living that way. Considering Jessie's budget for renovating a house when she could buy a new one twice the size for the same price, maybe none of them needed to work at all and were born million-aires.

Turning back to the matter at hand, he reminded Michael that all the usual rules for visiting people applied with Jessie.

"I know, Dad. No visiting if I haven't finished my home-work and chores. Always let you know when I'm leaving and when I'll return. If the weather is bad, you'll come pick me up when it's time to come home. And always be polite."

"You got it. And, uh, in her case, don't allow her dog to use you as a chew toy," Galen joked as he tickled his son, send-ing him into peals of laughter.

Freed to finally visit Jessie again, Michael quickly fin-ished his chores and homework for the weekend then he headed over as fast as his and Kipper's feet could carry them.

He found her sitting outside on the front porch steps, Causy lying beside her. She was bundled up in a suede coat with her gloves on and looked as if she was about to leave.

"Hey, Jessie. My dad said it was okay for me to visit you now that you've met. I hope now is okay?" He asked, trying not to sound disappointed as he noticed the keys in her hand.

"Of course, honey, you can come see me anytime. I always have time for a friend." Despite her smile, he thought she looked like she'd been about to cry.

"Cool!" He plopped down beside her on the stairs, sitting a little close since it was chilly. "So what are you doing?"

She chuckled. "To be honest, I'm being the world's biggest chicken. I need to get groceries and Causy needs more food, but I'm too scared to get in the car and drive to the store."

"Is it because of how you're scared of people's reaction to your eye?"

"Yep. You know, after I first got hurt, I wasn't so scared. I just ignored anybody staring or whispering, told myself they weren't talking about me and that I was just over thinking things." She paused and looked at him. "You know how sometimes if you are feeling kinda sad, you want to just sit and eat your favorite foods?"

"Oh yeah, I love eating macaroni and cheese."

"Me too, I love mac and cheese." She smiled again and nudged his shoulder. "Or a nice bowl of cheesy grits. Well, one day I was feeling pretty down, so I decided to go to my favorite Italian restaurant to get stuffed pasta shells, which is another of my favorite foods. But while I was there, the manager asked me to leave because the other people were getting sick looking at me, said it made it so they couldn't eat and so they wanted me to go away."

"What!? No way!" He exclaimed, shocked to hear adults could be as mean as kids sometimes. "That is so mean! You shouldn't have to leave just because some people were so rude."

Jessie hugged his shoulders with a smile. "Thanks, and I know you're right. But at the time, it hurt so much I couldn't tell them that. I just left without another word. Afterward, I noticed the staring more, and it got to the point it felt like everyone was talking about me with disgusted expressions on their faces. Eventually, I couldn't go anywhere because I was scared of being hurt again. I tried covering my eye with these glasses, but people still stared, so I finally reached the point where I can't leave the house at all, unless I'm in the car the whole time. That day we met in the cemetery, I'd been sitting in the car half an hour trying to get out, even though no one else was there."

"Oh, wow. I think I can understand why you got scared, but it has to be kinda boring to be stuck in the house all the time, and if you don't go anywhere, how will you get food and stuff?"

"Well, last time my big brother James brought it for me. I could call him now and he'd have more over here within an hour. But I wanted to try shopping by myself this time." A gust of wind made them both shiver. "Now I really wish I had been brave enough to go, then I could make us some nice hot chocolate to chase away this chill."

Michael hated the thought of his friend being stuck at home, scared of people just because of some bullies. But he also knew how hard it could be to fight fear. He thought back to the cemetery and was doubly glad he'd approached her, since it helped her say goodbye to Mr. Clark. Maybe he could help her again like that now, the way his dad used to. "Hey, you know when the fair comes in the fall, they have all these haunted houses and stuff. They looked kind of fun, but I was too scared to go into them. Well, one year, my dad said he would lend me his strength, so we could fight the fear together. He held my hand and we walked all the way through one. I was still scared, but it wasn't as bad. Maybe I could lend you my strength and we can go to the store together?"

"Maybe...maybe...would be worth a try, right? But would your dad be okay with you going to the store with me?"

"Let me call and ask him." They headed inside where Michael called to ask permission. Not wanting to embarrass Jessie with the truth, he explained that they wanted to make hot chocolate, but she was out of milk and marshmallows. It wasn't exactly a fib, as she was out of those things too. To his relief, his dad agreed.

"He said it's fine, just make sure to wear our seatbelts and drive safe." Michael held out his hand with a smile. "Come on, let's go be brave."

With the dogs safely locked in the house, they headed out. As they pulled into the grocery store parking lot, the sign seemed to loom like a monster above them, and Jessie could feel the tremors start. Michael grabbed her hand and reminded her he was there and that it would be okay. Nodding, Jessie gave his hand a light squeeze then made herself get out. He met her at the back of the car and thrust his small hand into hers, holding on with a surprisingly firm grip.

They slowly walked across the parking lot. Though there was no one walking around outside at the time, it still took everything in her to not turn around and run back to the safety of the car.

Inside, as they grabbed a cart, she stopped to take several deep breaths, but Michael's grip remained firm and they steered the cart together. As they made their way through the produce section, Jessie was certain she could feel a few people staring at her and thought she heard whispers from behind. The tension tightened in her back, and she froze. Tremors started running through her body again.

"It's okay, no one is saying anything mean, I promise." Michael whispered and gave her hand another squeeze. "Actually, they sound kinda happy to see you."

Telling herself that such a sweet boy wouldn't lie, she nodded and managed to keep going. It was slow, but somehow they made it through the lightly trafficked store and had a cart loaded with stuff. The checkouts were the hardest part, but fortunately, the young clerk wasn't anyone who knew

Jessie. Without even looking up at them, she gave them a half-hearted auto greeting as she started ringing up the groceries.

Back at the SUV, with the groceries loaded, Jessie sat with her hands on the steering wheel a moment, taking a few deep breaths. "I…we…we did it, didn't we?"

"Yep, you did it, Jessie! You did great!"

Laughing, she gladly accepted the hug he offered and asked, "Should we test our luck by going to the pet store too?"

"Yeah, let's go. You can do it!"

Bolstered by the boy's infectious enthusiasm, she drove them down the block to the local pet store. It was a shorter trip to an even emptier store due to the time of day. They quickly grabbed two huge bags of food and some treats and made it back to the car. Once they returned to the house and everything was unloaded, they celebrated with the promised hot chocolate and homemade strawberry muffins.

Chapter 14

OVER DINNER, GALEN ASKED Michael how his visit with Jessie had gone.

"It was fun! After we went to the store and had our hot chocolate, she showed me how to teach Kipper to lay down. She said he's a smart puppy and I should be able to teach him lots. Want to see?"

"Maybe after we finish eating," Galen replied with a smile, knowing his son would otherwise abandon his plate to show off Kipper's new trick. And right now, he wanted to get to the bottom of the comments he'd heard earlier. "You know son, I heard a few people talking about your trip to town with Jessie."

"Oh?" Michael's eyes dropped to his plate and he began taking bites in rapid succession, which only confirmed Galen's instincts that his son was hiding something.

"Yep. Seems it's the first time anyone has seen Jessie out in public since she moved here. Seems hard to believe anyone could go over a month without driving into town at all. Then I started thinking about how nervous she was when I saw her, and you asking if I'd done something to make her scared of me. Wondered if maybe you knew something about that?"

Michael chewed his lip. Galen knew he was being a little unfair. It was one thing for Michael to hide something, but not answering honestly would be a full out lie, which wasn't something Galen would let slide as easily.

"It wasn't really the first time, though, I guess it was the first time going into town. She went to see Mr. Clark's grave too and say goodbye to him. I guess I kind of know why, but you told me it was wrong to gossip and share people's private businesses, so that's why I didn't say anything."

"Good, I'm glad you are respecting her privacy. But remember how we talked about good secrets and bad secrets?"

"Yeah, bad ones are ones I should tell you or another grown up about, because someone might need help."

"Right. So, would you say this is a good one or a bad one?"

"I'm not sure. It isn't something good like a surprise party or a gift, but I don't think Jessie is in trouble, or at least, not the kind like we talked about." Galen waited patiently while Michael thought it through. He wanted Michael to grow up with a strong sense of ethics and personal responsibility, and while he didn't want his son to think keeping any secret was okay, he also didn't want to force the boy to tell him more than he was comfortable with sharing about Jessie, or something she might not want shared. Though he couldn't imagine she'd tell a ten-year-old a huge secret, it was clear she had told him something.

"Well, the thing is, she isn't scared of you, at least not just you." Michael finally said aloud. "You've seen her glasses, right?"

"Yes, they are rather unique. I noticed she had scars around her eye, so I presumed she had an accident while living up north?"

"Kind of." Michael squirmed in his chair a bit, then nodded as if to himself. "See, there was a bad man and he took her eye and now it's broken and can't be fixed. But it made her face scarred and while she was out, people were mean and said nasty things. Even her favorite restaurant made her leave because they said her face was disgusting to look at. So, she got really scared of people and going out because she is afraid they will bully her again. She was even scared to go to Mr. Clark's grave, but she managed to drive there. To be honest, I saw her there, and I ended up helping her find it. I didn't know she was scared to go by herself at the time. So, I'm helping her get better because she's my friend and that's what friends do, right?"

While he was proud of his son's declaration, it greatly bothered Galen to think someone had "taken" her eye. Michael was too young to really think about the ramifications of that kind of incident, but Galen knew it must have been a pretty bad situation. Maybe an abusive boyfriend or a random mugging gone wrong. Still, it explained her behavior at their meeting better.

"So, is that the real reason y'all went to the store together?"

"Well, she really did need groceries and wanted to make us hot chocolate. But when I got to her house, she was stuck outside. So I said I'd go with her, like you did to help me get through the haunted houses at the fair. And it worked! We made it through the whole store and the pet store too." Michael sounded rightly proud of Jessie's achievement.

"That is good to hear, son, and I'm proud of you for helping her. Not a lot of people would be strong enough to do that, you know."

"Thanks, Dad." Michael's smile slipped to a frown. "Does this make me a gossip now?"

"No, not at all. You're being a good friend to her and I'm glad you told me. Now I can help her too by being mindful of her fears while I work on her house. Besides, since you two are becoming such good friends, I think it would be good if she and I could become friends too, right?"

"Yeah! I'll make sure to put in a good word for you! Now that I know she isn't scared of only you, she's bound to like you. After all, you're pretty cool, I mean for a dad and all."

GALEN CALLED JESSIE FRIDAY afternoon, as promised, with an update on the proposal. He still had a few quotes outstanding on some of the more specialty items but expected those in by the end of Monday, at the latest. So they set a date and time to meet the following week.

For once, since Jessie's arrival, Michael was excited about something else when Galen came home. Namely, the two-day police dog exhibition happening in Rela over the weekend. The event was held jointly by the various police forces in the area in which K-9 handlers participated in a friendly competition to showcase their dog partners' training and skills.

Michael had looked so forward to it that he went to bed without being asked, and was up bright and early, eager to get going. His excitement was infectious, so Galen even agreed to leave a little earlier than necessary. As they pulled out of the drive, Michael asked if they could invite Jessie. Galen suspected she'd decline due to her issues with leaving the house, but to their mutual surprise, her SUV was nowhere in sight when they stopped by.

The field where the competition was being held was part of a large county park that contained multiple sports fields for local teams to play on, with pine copses nestled between them and a mix of pines, maples, and oaks in the forest circling the area. White metal bleachers had been set up around one of the soccer fields, which had been repurposed to hold the competition. One side of the field had a series of obstacle jumps set up, while the other had a ring sprayed out on the grass. Sun soaked the sky, but even its bright rays couldn't keep the fall chill out of the air and most people there were wearing jackets and long sleeve shirts

When they arrived, they looked for Phillip, who had gone ahead with some other officers from the Cascade Falls force. The town had three police dogs, courtesy of the Bradshaw generosity, and all three were slated to participate. They found him standing near one of the fields where the events would be held, talking to another officer.

"Hey bro, hey kiddo!" Phillip waved and waited for them to join him. "Excited to see the dogs in action?"

"Of course, where are they?" Michael answered while scanning for the area for dogs, the objects of his obsession.

Laughing, Galen remarked that Michael had thoroughly educated him on everything a ten-year-old could learn about police dogs over the past week.

Phillip laughed as well. "Well, before your head starts spinning around from all that excitement, come on. We have time to go peek at the kennel area."

"Cool!"

When they arrived, they were surprised to see Jessie there, her big dog in tow. She stood talking to her brother Julian in front of the row of tall metal kennels. Galen thought she looked pale and nervous, and she seemed to move closer to Julian as she saw them approaching before recognizing them and relaxing a touch.

"Jessie!" Michael called as he ran towards her and enveloped her in a hug. "I didn't know you were coming to see the competition too?"

Jessie smiled down at the boy and returned the hug. "Hey. I hadn't planned on it, but I needed to help out an old friend of mine."

"An old friend?"

Before she could answer, hideous growls mixed with threatening barks came from inside the kennel near them. Jessie quietly slipped Michael behind her and moved them both away from the kennels towards Galen. After checking Michael was okay, Galen looked at the black German Shepherd still raging inside the kennel.

"What set him off?"

Before Jessie answered, Michael piped up. "Isn't that Thor?"

"Yes, yes, it is," Jessie replied.

"When he came to our school, he was really nice. We all pet him and even played with him. He works with Officer Maxwell, right? He probably won't like him acting like that."

Jessie looked at Galen with a sad expression, then glanced back down at Michael. "I…" she started to say, then looked at Galen again as if seeking permission. He nodded, trusting she would explain whatever she needed to say appropriately. Squatting down to Michael's level, she put a hand on Michael's shoulder.

"Well, you see honey, last week Officer Maxwell was helping some county officers chase two bank robbers over in Granville County. They caught up to the men, but well, the men didn't really want to be arrested so they shot at the officers."

"Did the officers get hurt?"

"Yes, some of them did, including Officer Maxwell."

"But I thought police dogs like Thor protected cops from bad guys, so that way cops don't get hurt?"

"They do or at least they try. Thor did his best, but the men shot him too."

"Oh…but Officer Maxwell will be okay, right?"

Galen moved closer, already knowing the answer. He'd read about the shooting in the news, and only just now put it together with the dog in the kennel.

"No honey, he won't. I'm afraid he died."

Michael stared at her a moment. "Does that mean he's in heaven like my momma?"

"Yes, yes it does." Jessie gave him another hug as the boy began crying. She held him close and rubbed his back. Galen squatted down behind Michael and added his own touch to hers to comfort his son. Once the tears stopped, she looked toward the kennel. "Since then, Thor has been scared and confused. He doesn't understand what's happening and being hurt has left him kind of mixed up. That is making him act aggressively and he won't let anyone near him."

"I think I understand." Michael said with a sniffle. "After Mom died, I didn't want anyone around me either."

Galen stood up behind Michael. "Why is he here at the competition? I can't imagine he's participating when he's acting like that?"

Jessie shook her head. "No, he isn't. Some officers from Granville transported him here from their vet office so he can be taken back to Cascade Falls. As I was the person who initially raised and trained him, I'm taking him into my custody to try to help him get better."

Galen was surprised such a thing was being allowed, though he supposed her being who she was had likely helped. "He seems pretty dangerous, are you sure he won't hurt you?" Galen also gave a meaningful glance down at Michael.

"He won't. When we're alone, he doesn't act like this, which is why I'm going to try to rehabilitate him. He clearly remembers me, and while he is a little skittish, he allows me to handle him. It's mostly a matter of helping him trust the rest of the world again."

In some ways Thor sounded like Jessie and Galen wondered if in trying to help the dog she was hoping to help herself. Much like fixing up an old house might be too. Still, it bothered him to think a clearly dangerous animal would be on her property.

As if reading his mind, Jessie straightened. "You don't need to worry. Except when I'm working with him, he'll be locked in a large enclosure. When he is outside his pen, he will be muzzled as an extra precaution."

Galen nodded, hoping she didn't take his concern as an insult. It was obvious she cared for his son and Galen was certain she'd never willingly put him in danger.

Phillip interrupted to note things would be started soon and they had better find some seats. Grateful for the unexpected save, he agreed and with a polite "see you later" to Jessie and Julian, he ushered Michael towards the spectator stands. Before they had gone far, Michael turned and ran back to Jessie, calling out to her.

"Um, Jessie, would you like to sit with us?"

Jessie glanced back at Julian, who'd already started walking towards the parking lot before Michael's voice had stopped him. Galen could almost feel the indecision between wanting to flee and not wanting to disappoint the grinning boy holding his hand out for her.

Finally, she gave him a smile and took his hand. "I think I'd like that, if you don't mind a shaky thing like me beside you." Julian declined to join them, as he was still on duty. As they continued, Galen fell into step beside her and leaned towards her just a bit, so he wouldn't be overheard.

"I'm sorry if I implied that you would endanger Michael. I hadn't meant it like that."

"I know." She whispered back with another smile. "Thank you for trusting me with him." Reaching the bleachers around the field, Phillip led them towards an area right in the middle, so they could be high enough up that Michael would be able to see. Somehow, Jessie ended up sitting between Michael and Galen, with Causy laying herself across the seat in front. They certainly didn't have to worry about anyone trying to sit directly in front of them now. Galen heard Michael whisper, "You're doing good, Jessie."

Galen had seen Michael grab Jessie's hand and after quietly watching them a few minutes, he remembered Michael mentioning the haunted houses and realized why his son was holding her hand so tight. Galen could feel she was still trembling though. Not wanting to freak her out even more but also hating the thought of her spending the whole time afraid, Galen quietly turned his hand up in silent invitation. Seeing the movement, Jessie looked down at his hand, then back up at him. He gave her what he hoped was a reassuring smile.

For a moment, he was certain she would decline the invitation, but slowly, she moved her hand towards his, hesitating before letting her fingers touch the palm of his. Galen didn't dare move as she wrestled with herself a moment before fully placing her hand in his. Very carefully, he closed his hand over hers, inordinately pleased when she didn't pull away, but instead squeezed his hand. Even better, the trembles eased and she gave him a shaky smile.

As the event got underway, she lost the fearful, hesitant look, smiled more freely, and seemed to be enjoying herself. He also found that she was a wealth of information about the competition, answering his questions about the different events and how they were scored. Chatting about the dogs made her come alive, and somewhere along the way Galen realized that she was a beautiful woman when she wasn't being eaten up by fear, even with those quirky glasses. By the time they parted ways after the day's events were over, he found himself anticipating working on the Clark house with her.

Chapter 16

After the exhibition, Jessie left with Thor while Galen and Michael stopped in Sylva for dinner at Speedy's Pizza before continuing home. Michael had talked nearly non-stop about the event since they'd left, but he was finally starting to wind down. He took his bath without any fuss and fell asleep almost as soon as his head hit the pillow.

After turning off his son's light, Galen headed back downstairs to pour himself a brandy before relaxing in the living room. Designed with a child in mind, the gray sofa and matching armchair were sturdily constructed and covered in stain-resistant microfiber. A large low table sat in front of the sofa, ideal for doing homework or playing games. Beside the armchair was a small round mahogany table for drinks, books, and the like.

The large comfortable armchair was Galen's favorite brooding place, and he sat in it now, swirling the amber liquor in his glass as he thought about holding hands with Jessie earlier. The touch of her warm hand had sent shivers over his palm and up his wrist. He curled his fingers, hoping the sensation would go away. He couldn't feel this way, not about her. Not about the lady who was guarded and feared him days earlier. But she was nice to his son and Michael clearly enjoyed being around her.

Why had he made the impulsive gesture? Sweat beaded his neck and his heartbeat increased as he thought back to her soft hand in his. He had only wanted to comfort her. Right? He'd helped ease her fear, same as he would anyone. So why hadn't he let go of her hand once she seemed okay? Her little smiles had done things to his mind, and that first full, true smile had him smiling back even now. He couldn't help himself.

Restless, he stood, walked over to the fireplace, and leaned against the wood mantle before throwing back the rest of his drink. The back of his throat burned. Tears came to his eyes as he stared at the picture of Melinda in her wedding gown. Her long blonde hair had been piled high that day, with a riot of wispy curls cascading down her back. During the reception after the wedding, those curls had driven him to distraction, teasing him. Melinda had known just how crazy it drove him, so whenever she saw him watching her, she'd given her head a little shake to taunt him with the dangling tresses. At the motel, where they spent the night before going on their honeymoon, they'd barely made it through the door before he freed the curls from the pins to bury his hands in her hair.

Melinda. He'd developed a crush on her the first day of high school, a crush that had rapidly turned into a deep connection, a friendship that had morphed into love. Despite both sets of parents strongly urging them to date others before committing, they married in their junior year of college. Two years later, Michael was born. It had been tough at times, with both working their way through college while balancing bills and a baby. Their parents, having accepted their marriage and loving to dote on their grandson, had been a godsend. After years of hard work, Galen established his name in the renovation business and Melinda had finished up her coursework, which would allow her to become a fully licensed, non-provisional real estate agent.

One obscenely gorgeous Sunday morning, Melinda had been making pancakes while they talked about taking Michael to the zoo. Then she was on the floor, her legs had simply gone numb from under her and her vision started acting up. Galen rushed her to the hospital, and at first, the emergency room doctor thought she'd had a mild stroke, so they performed a CT scan. Then they came back and said they needed to do an MRI as well, though it had only been vaguely explained at the time as "needing to confirm something" they'd seen on the first test. He could still remember how his heart stopped when another doctor, an oncologist, entered the room, sat beside Melinda, held her hand, and told them she had a large tumor on her brain.

They'd tried to remain hopeful, but a biopsy confirmed the tumor was malignant. Their doctor has been honest with them from the beginning. With where the tumor was located, her chances of living more than a few years were slim at best, and that all they could really do was help try to maintain the quality of her life for as long as possible. In the end, they'd only had three years together after her initial diagnosis. The whole time, Melinda maintained a brave front with everyone, refusing to let the illness beat her before her time.

Her positive nature had made it easier on Michael when the time came. It had been hard to explain to him what was wrong with mommy, as he'd only been four at the time she was diagnosed, but they did their best while also trying not to expose him to the harsher effects of the illness. Galen was grateful that he and Michael were able to say goodbye the night she died. Michael had been heartbroken, of course, but her death had ripped Galen apart. For a while, knowing his son needed him was the only thing holding him together.

When Phillip suggested moving to Cascade Falls for a new start, Galen readily agreed, wanting to raise his son away from the city. He hadn't been able to leave Melinda behind; he'd had her body transferred to the Andrews family plot in town, so he and Michael could visit her whenever they wanted.

Since then, his primary focus had been raising his son and building his renovation business. Dating hadn't really entered his mind at all. He'd pointedly ignored the random attempts at flirting from some of the single females in town and his mom's occasional hints about some "nice girl" she'd met somewhere. Though Phillip even sometimes suggested he should go out, Galen just wasn't interested.

He honestly wasn't sure himself if it was out of a lingering devotion to Melinda's memory, or just not feeling much attraction to any of the choices around him at the time. It wasn't until Jessie became friends with Michael that he'd realized what his son had probably been wanting and needing— a good female presence in his life. Galen wasn't about to think of a new wife, but maybe his son was seeking something intangible in his friendship with Jessie that he should have been getting from Melinda.

His thoughts coming full circle, Galen realized he still hadn't figured out his own reaction to her. She was a beautiful woman, scars or no, but he refused to think about that. As he replaced Melinda's picture, he murmured, "It was only a friendly gesture. The same as I would've done for a scared child." By the time he headed to bed, he'd almost manage to convince himself that that was really all it was.

Down the street, Jessie mirrored many of Galen's actions. Her drink of choice was a glass of milk, joined by a rich, gooey brownie, for extra comfort, and her brooding seat was a large red armchair in her bedroom, with Causy stretched out on her cushion at the foot of the bed. She'd already showered and changed into a sleeveless white nightgown with faint pink and green flowers down to her ankles. She loved the simple style and the softness of the fabric, and it was one of the only sleeveless or even short sleeved items she'd kept from her old wardrobe. Something she could indulge in while alone and no one could see.

Studying her bare arms impartially, she knew she was too thin. She hadn't regained much of the weight she lost during the long stay at the hospital and the months after where she'd eaten only out of necessity or when reminded rather than from any desire to provide sustenance to her body. It left her fingers small, her wrists sharp and bony. Of course, that was easier to overlook than the dozens of white scars of varying lengths and widths running up and down both arms. For a moment, she could see the flash of a knife as it slid across her skin. She pushed the image away, taking several deep breaths before quickly gulping some milk.

Leaning back in the chair with a sigh, she let her mind wander back to the events today. She should be thinking about how to get started with Thor, but instead, she kept seeing Galen's upturned hand beside her, quietly offering his strength the way his son so easily had. He hadn't made a big show of it, just moved it slightly and turned it upwards so she knew it was there. Had her fear been so palpable or had she looked pathetic? Shaking her head, she ordered herself to stop trying to find something negative behind Galen's gift. He hadn't laughed, hadn't given her a frustrated or disgusted look. He'd just given her that sweet smile.

More surprising to her was that she'd accepted. She'd hesitated at first, not wanting to be gripped with the terror that a man's touch usually brought. But that time, the terrors hadn't come. Instead, his hand had felt so warm. And while he had calluses from his construction work, somehow, his hand still had a pleasant softness to it. What would his hands feel like elsewhere? Shocked to have thought that, she shook her head. *Where had that come from?* Since the attack, she hadn't seen men in that way at all; they'd only been monsters, horrible things to avoid, except her brothers.

She'd never have imagined she could feel any sort of attraction for a man again. Was she attracted to Galen? Was that what this feeling was? He was a successful, intelligent man, with a quiet strength about him. Knowing Michael, it was obvious Galen was a wonderful father, raising his son to be well-mannered and well-behaved, but also teaching him the importance of making his own decisions and of being responsible for those decisions.

Being honest, yes, she felt some attraction towards Galen. Not that it mattered. He may be friendly with her because she was friends with his son, but a man like that could never feel physical desire for a woman like her. Standing, she walked into the bathroom to stare into one of the only mirrors left in the house. She'd removed the rest and tossed them in the attic not long after moving in.

Hand shaking slightly, she removed the glasses, uncovering the scar that ran from the right edge of her left eyebrow diagonally down through her eye and just a little past the socket. The doctors had done their best, but the wound had been too deep to save her eye and what was left didn't resemble an eye much anymore, just a strange, scarred-up wasteland on her face. Sure, it looked better than it had at first, when the scar had still been red and raw, but it certainly wasn't anything someone would want to wake up to, turn over, and see. Hell, it was her face and she didn't like to look at it.

It was another reason she'd had her glasses custom made. The design was based on a similar pair worn by the central character in the Gungrave anime series, who'd also lost one of his eyes. In his case, it had been from being shot directly in that eye rather than slashed by a knife. As she had no actual vision issues, well beyond the whole missing an eye thing, the clear right lens was just plain plastic with a mild UV protective coating added. Since she'd gotten the glasses, she wore them constantly, only removing them after climbing into bed or to clean the lenses. The minute she woke up, she'd put them back on before moving.

So far, Galen had only seen the edges of the scar, the bits not covered by the glasses. That alone would turn off any man, and that was before seeing her arms or the many other scars left behind by that psychopath eight months ago. Again, a memory tried to push forward causing the inevitable trembles in her hands. Her breathing quickened, as if she was again in that dark room, desperate to escape.

"NO, I will not subject myself to this!" She yelled aloud as she ruthlessly shoved the memory away, stalking out of the bathroom to retrieve her milk and the brownie. Not wanting to return to her fanciful thoughts of Galen either, she took her evening snack and left the room.

As she walked out of the bedroom, Causy quietly got up and followed. Jessie went downstairs to the home office and settled at her desk while Causy plopped down in the cushy dog bed beside it. Finishing off the brownie, Jessie opened one of her favorite historical strategy games and spent several hours chasing away bad memories and impossible dreams.

Chapter 17

AFTER BREAKFAST JESSIE and Causy headed outside to the kennel to feed Thor his breakfast and have their first session together. Thor stood at attention, watching them approach, his posture stiff. Tension radiated from him, like a coiled spring waiting to be released.

When they were a few feet from the kennel, he began barking and snarling much as he had done the day before at the exhibition. Jessie stopped then began walking backwards, Causy remaining at heel. As soon as Thor ceased raging at them, she stopped again and put Causey into a sit-stay, then slowly walked forward again. He watched her carefully but remained quiet.

"Good boy," she said quietly. "So even other dogs aren't friends right now, are they?" With careful movements, she sat down in front of the door, the bowl of food in her hands. "Now, I need to feed you, but that display you just made makes it hard to trust I can open that door. And yeah, I could slide it in the bottom, but that isn't going to get us anywhere, so how about we just talk a bit, how about that?"

Continuing in the same soft, easy voice she began babbling about the weather, the town, her work, anything that came to mind. As she talked, she eased bits of kibble into the kennel. The first few pieces fell to the concrete floor where Thor sniffed them as thoroughly as a cat before finally eating them.

After several rounds of this, he moved closer to where she was putting the kibble in. She held her hand beside the wire, where he could lick the kibble off her hand but kept it relatively safe from a potential bite. Cautiously, Thor stuck out his tongue and lapped off a piece, darting back almost immediately. Moments later he crept back to her hand and repeated the procedure, but he didn't go as far. By the fifth piece, he was staying at the fence, eating calmly.

"That's a good boy. Don't suppose you want to lie down for me." She kept her voice even, rather than injecting the command at a louder voice. He whined and sat, then waited for more kibble. "That's not a down, but we'll call it a start," she said with a small smile and offered up another handful.

"To be honest, boy, I'm winging this. I've read up a lot on dealing with aggressive dogs and I'm going to adapt some of those techniques for you. I know you're scared. Your friend died, and you got hurt while doing your job." As she talked, she continued feeding him kibble, glad to see his ears moving at the sound of her voice. He was unlikely to understand most of her words, but he was listening and that was all she wanted. "People did that to you, and so you decided people are now monstrous things to be feared. And when you're scared, your mind goes to flight or fight mode. Me, I run, you, you fight. But still, we're a lot alike, you and me. My family hasn't given up on me yet, and I'm not giving up on you. So let's do this, boy, let's get better together, eh?"

The last of the kibble offered, she held her empty hand up against the wire. After a moment, he gave it a lick and his tail moved in the briefest of wags. It was a small movement, but it was the first truly friendly sign he'd given her since she'd taken custody of him. That was a good enough start for her.

"Yeah, you're still a good boy. We can do this." Keeping her movements small and slow, she stood again and wiped her hand on her jeans. "I need to get to work now, but I'll be back this evening. Get some sleep, we got work to do."

Jessie headed back around to the front of the house, Causy falling into heel position as soon as she reached her. It hurt seeing the dog she'd known so long being so afraid and acting so violently. As a puppy, Thor had been bright, easy to train, and a love machine. Nothing made him happier than a good petting session and he'd preferred a "good dog" with lots of gentle ear rubs to food as a reward.

There'd been worries he'd fail his police dog training because he was so sweet natured, but it hadn't taken him too long to understand the difference between "cop" and "criminal," and that the latter were threats to the people who would give him all the petting he could ask for. But even after learning to attack and defend his officer, he'd remained friendly in general and had been the favorite of the force's three dogs to act as the social ambassador. The other two dogs were both good, of course, but Thor had that special spark that made him a crowd hit.

His fans wouldn't even recognize him versus the tightly wound, ready to attack dog now sitting in Jessie's kennel. As she sat at her desk, she spared a dark thought for the men who'd hurt Thor and killed Officer Maxwell. She knew they would likely spend life in prison for their crimes, but if she couldn't find a way to help him, Thor would be paying for those men's crimes with his life.

Chapter 18

ON THURSDAY, GALEN CAME by to review the write-up for the renovation project. While she was still nervous, Jessie was much less afraid than the first time and able to meet him at the door without shaking.

"Good morning." She greeted him with a smile and held the door open for him to come in.

"Morning." Galen returned the smile as she led him into the kitchen.

"Coffee?" she offered as she fixed herself a cup. As he accepted, she realized her nervous feeling wasn't from the usual fears, rather it was in being with him specifically. After handing him his cup and setting sugar and cream out on the table, she joined him. "Oh, um, I never did thank you for the other day, at the competition. I, um, I really appreciated it."

Another smile. The man was gorgeous when he smiled. "Oh, it's okay. I'm glad it helped. It was a fun competition and Michael had a ball. How are things going with Thor?"

"To be honest, it's been mixed. In the morning, we do bonding exercises, where I mostly just talk to him while sitting near him and offer him a pet if he wants it. Then in the evenings, I take him through all the basic training routines he did as a puppy. I'm hoping to remind him how much he is loved and to help him see that he is safe now. He's doing well there, but he's also continuing to be aggressive towards Causy, which is a much less promising sign." She sighed. "Still, it's early. I knew we could be looking at months of work to bring him back around."

"Wow, it's hard to imagine him being so messed up he'd try to challenge a dog as big as her." Galen frowned. "What kind of chance does he have of being cured?"

"It's hard to tell. With a typical pet dog, animal behaviorists have seen aggression issues resolved with pretty high success rates. Whether his police training will improve his odds or make it harder though, I don't know."

"At least he's in good hands, if the progress I've seen with Kipper is any indication. By the way, thanks for helping Michael train him. I'd been thinking for a while that he needed some obedience work but had no clue where to start. I hope we aren't taking advantage of your kindness though. I know dog training isn't generally a free thing."

Jessie laughed. "No, it's fine. I love working with them and Michael is a joy to have around. He is a sweet kid and learns fast. Really, I'm just showing him how to do it. He's doing all the hard work of practicing. Besides, he apparently had the same idea as you and insisted he 'pay' for the training himself, so we agreed he'd help me work on the garden."

With Michael visiting almost every day as soon as he was done with his homework, they'd had plenty of time to both run Kipper through his paces and to start working on the fenced in beds where Jessie planned to plant some winter vegetables.

"That sounds like a good deal." Galen beamed clearly proud of his son. She could get addicted to those smiles. "I know he loves come over here, but honestly, if he starts interrupting your work or anything, just let us know. I know we haven't really set any kind of boundaries for his visits."

"No worries. He is always conscientious about asking if I'm busy when he comes by, and I let him know what times I work with Thor so he knows not to come around then. My work hours are very flexible, so usually when he comes by I'm ready for a break anyway."

"That's handy. Guessing you're self-employed?" Galen asked, using the opportunity to try to find out more about her.

"Yep. I'm a researcher, mostly running background checks and the like. Databases don't really care what time of day you access them," she replied, smoothly leaving off who she did the checks for. Most people would presume they were for employment checks. That they did them for anyone moving to the town was something kept quiet, revealed only when needed to confront the person about something found in those checks.

"Oh cool. That does sound like a great job for setting your own hours. Hopefully that will mean we can minimize disruptions to your work while we're doing with the renovations." Galen opened the folder he brought with him, reluctantly turning the conversation to the real reason for his visit. "With everything we discussed, and adding in some wiggle room for weather delays, we should be able to complete the entire project in eight months. We'll start with the outside areas first: the driveway, porch, siding, and roof, as well as the windows, before moving to the interior renovations."

He walked her through the itemized cost estimates and timeline breakdown, as well as the initial mockups for the kitchen remodel. Even with the more expensive materials she'd requested in some parts of the renovation, the cost estimate was well within her admittedly high budget.

"This all looks great. Thank you for putting it together so quickly." She said as she finished reading the contract and signed where he indicated.

"No problem. To be honest, I've wanted to work on this house for years, so I'm really excited to get started." He replied honestly. Remembering his discussion with Michael, he decided to take a chance on touching on the issue of her fears. "You should probably know, Michael shared your fears with me about going out in public. He didn't do it blindly, I kind of pulled it out of him, so I hope you won't be mad at him about it."

Jessie shook her head. "No, not at all. I'd kind of suspected he had when you offered me your hand at the competition, but then he told me he had himself and apologized for it. I already let him know it was okay. I wouldn't expect him to keep secrets from you or anything like that."

"Thank you. With that in mind, would I be wrong in thinking this project is going to be hard for you, with having my crews around?"

"Honestly, yes. The very thought terrifies the hell out of me. But I know I can't live like this forever. I'm hoping that being able to get to the store is a good sign that I'll be able to handle this too."

"Is there anything I can do to make it easier? Like introduce you to the crew members or anything?"

"Starting the work outside will help some, I think. Gives me time to get used to everyone being around before they start the inside work. Other than that, I can't really think of anything. I think it does help knowing that it's you leading this project, though," Jessie replied honestly, then blushed as she realized how that could sound. "I mean, because I know you are probably pretty particular about your crew and you're a good guy and..." Her voice trailed off as she dug herself deeper into the hole of embarrassment.

Galen blushed himself. "Thank you. And I promise, I check everyone out thoroughly before they go on my crew, so yeah, they are good guys. Besides, one look at Causy there, and they will probably be more afraid of you than you are of them."

They shared a laugh over that image. After Jessie wrote the check for the initial deposit and they confirmed a few final details, Jessie walked him to the front door.

"I guess I'll see you first thing Monday morning." Jessie held out her hand.

With a heart-throbbing grin, Galen shook her hand. His grip was as firm and warm as she remembered, and she was still smiling as she leaned against the porch pillar and watched him drive away.

Chapter 19

EARLY SATURDAY, MICHAEL arrived bright and early to go with her to the garden center to pick out plants. Rather than the usual bone-deep fear, Jessie was grateful to find herself feeling just mild anxiety. Enough to still be there, but not enough to kill her excitement about shopping for the plants and the fun she would have spending time with Michael. She fixed them some travel mugs filled with hot chocolate to enjoy on the trip, as the garden center was a bit outside of town. Once they were on the road, Michael asked her how Thor was doing.

"It's tough to say. He acts fine in my training sessions with me, but he keeps raging at Causy if she gets too near his kennel. During one of our training sessions, while on his long lead, he tried to attack her."

"Really?! That's crazy!"

"Yeah, it surprised me. Fortunately, he was muzzled at the time, and Causy didn't fight back. She just pinned him down and waited for me to deal with it."

Michael went quiet for a few minutes, then asked in a low voice. "Hey Jessie, what will happen if he doesn't get better?"

She'd hoped he wouldn't ask, as she knew the truth would hurt him, but she also didn't want to lie to him. "Well sweetie, he's a large, powerful dog and has shown that he will attack anyone without provocation because he is so afraid. That makes him very dangerous. If I can't help him get his fear under control enough for it to be safe for him to live a normal life, he'll have to be euthanized so he doesn't hurt anyone or himself."

"Oh…" Michael looked down at his lap. "I really hope you can help him then. He was such a good dog before. Think it will help if I include him in my prayers at night?"

Jessie ruffled his hair and smiled. "Certainly can't hurt."

Once they reached the garden center, they headed for the vegetable and herb area. Jessie picked up seedlings of spinach, broccoli, several kinds of lettuce, carrots, cabbage, and onions. Near the end of the vegetable section, Jessie started looking at Brussel sprouts, much to Michael's disgust.

"Eww, you like those?"

"Oh, I love them, especially cooked in garlic butter. You don't like them?"

"No way. They are so bitter and tough!"

"Ah, if they are bitter, then they haven't been cooked right. Maybe when they sprout, you'll try the ones I make and see if you might like them more?"

"Ummm…we'll see." Jessie couldn't help laughing at how he scrunched up his face. After picking up some herbs, they headed over to the flower and plant section to find some pretty bushes and grasses to put in the beds that were out of the construction areas, as well as bulbs and seeds to plant for spring blooms. They oohed and awed over the colorful asters and laughed at the funny faces of the pansies as they added flats to their cart. They also picked up chrysanthemums, lobelia, and some decorative cabbage. For plants that wouldn't come up until spring, they picked out a variety of crocus, daffodils, dahlias, daylilies, tulips, and poppies. They were nearly done when Michael stopped to stare at a large display of irises.

"Jessie, are these flowers we could plant now?"

"Yes, I think so. It looks like these have been started so they can still be placed in the ground now."

"Um, do you think maybe we could plant some of these? These were my mom's favorite flowers."

"Of course. What colors do you think she'd like?"

"Hmmm." Using the pictures on the plant's tags, he selected some in a vibrant blue variety that had a lighter shade of the same blue running through the petals, a pretty purple bearded iris with touches of yellow in the center, and one that was a blend of rusty brown and dark orange tones.

"Those are all very pretty. I'm sure she'll love them."

Michael nodded and thanked her. "Are you going to get any for you?"

"Well, I think I'll get this one here," she picked up one with lacy white petals tipped in a deep royal purple.

"Oh, I like that one too!"

Looking at their cart, Jessie frowned. "You know, we're gonna be exhausted by the time we get all these planted. Think we went a little overboard?"

Michael stared critically at the cart before answering. "Nah. We can do it. Maybe Causy and Kipper can help us dig?"

Laughing, Jessie pointed out that the holes they dug might not be quite the right ones for planting something in, which made Michael laugh as well. They were still chuckling as they checked out and headed out to the car to load everything into the back.

When they returned to Jessie's house, they left all the plants in the car and headed inside to enjoy some chicken noodle soup and grilled cheese sandwiches for lunch. They were just finishing up when someone knocked on the door. Startled, Jessie couldn't help jumping a little. Causy was on her feet in an instant and down the hall to investigate. Michael asked if she was expecting someone as they followed, but she could only shake her head no. Checking the peephole, she was both relieved and surprised to see Galen standing on the other side. She quickly let Causy know it was okay and opened the door to let Galen in.

"Hi, guys. Hope you don't mind me dropping in, I noticed you were back and thought you might like a hand with the planting." He grinned.

Jessie returned the smile, happier than she'd admit to his deciding to drop in for a social visit. "Sure, I certainly won't turn down the help. We might have gotten just a little happy at the store."

Galen followed them to Jessie's SUV. When she opened the back, his jaw dropped at the number of plants in the back. "A little happy? Did y'all leave anything behind?"

"The radishes!" Jessie and Michael answered together then broke out laughing. It was the one vegetable they'd both agreed could stay behind without complaints.

Shaking his head and smiling, Galen grabbed several flats. "So, where to?"

Jessie handed Michael an appropriately sized flat before picking up several herself, then led the way to the fenced in portion of the back garden. Several runs later, the vegetables and herbs were stacked and ready for planting there, while the flowers were waiting at the larger open area around the fenced part. By early evening, they managed to get everything planted and tucked into a healthy layer of cedar mulch.

To thank Galen and Michael for their hard work, Jessie offered to make dinner. The guys went home to clean up, agreeing to return in an hour. Jessie gave Thor a quick visit to feed him his dinner and give him some petting, which he accepted without any visible stress. That he continued to be calm with her was one thing that gave her hope of his being successfully reconditioned.

After showering and changing, she headed towards the kitchen then paused when she saw the message light on the home phone blinking. The first message was a hang-up as was the second. Her home number was unlisted, and her family would call her cell not the house phone. *He's in jail; there is no way he could call.* Checking the caller list, the numbers came up as unknown. Probably just a telemarketer then, she told herself firmly. There was no reason to think it was any-one else.

As she walked into the kitchen to start dinner, James called to check on her. She reassured him that she was doing well. When she told him about her dinner guests, he'd breathed an audible sound of relief and told her how proud he was of how far she'd come. She couldn't help being a little proud of herself, though more cautiously so. That was three trips to the store now, but still always with Michael.

She was more comfortable with Galen, even inviting him to dinner, but no one else yet. Giving herself a mental shake, she reminded herself that progress was progress, and she'd made more progress since she'd come home than she had in the months in Chicago after being released from the hospital.

Galen and Michael returned right on time. Leading them back to the kitchen, Galen offered to help, but Jessie shooed him to the table and asked them what they'd like to drink. After giving fruit juice to Michael and a glass of wine to Galen, she checked the ground beef browning for the sauce. They chatted about the garden while Jessie finished buttering several slices of Texas toast to make garlic bread. She'd visited Texas a few times and had picked up the technique of using the thick slices for both garlic bread and French toast. After rubbing it with fresh roasted garlic and laying on slices of mozzarella cheese, she set the bread aside to put in the oven when the pasta was done.

As the meat wasn't quite done yet, she went ahead and prepared Causy's dinner, carefully measuring the dry food into the large bowl. Having lain down near the kitchen door after the guys had arrived, Causy was on her feet the minute Jessie pulled the bowl out and followed her as she walked to the far wall of the kitchen. When they reached her feeding spot, Causy sat without Jessie saying a word, waiting patiently. Jessie put the bowl down at her feet and walked away, but the dog didn't move a muscle, watching Jessie instead of the bowl.

"Is she not hungry or something? She didn't pounce on you or act crazy at all while you're carrying the bowl and now she isn't eating?" Galen frowned in concern. He still couldn't say he liked the dog, but he didn't like to think she might be sick, as he knew it would hurt Jessie.

"No, she's fine. She's just waiting for permission to eat."

"Wow, seriously? Michael said she was well-trained, but that's wild! I wish Kipper would act half so calm. He nearly bowls Michael over at feeding time and he's not even full-grown yet."

"All a matter of training," she smiled at him. "As Causy is a trained guard dog, it's important for her not to eat anything just because it was put in front of her. So, she will only eat food she has expressed permission to touch." Galen watched in amazement as the dog continued to sit without twitching a muscle. He heard Jessie say a strange word and the dog began eating, calmly but rapidly.

"What was that you said? It didn't sound like 'eat'?"

"Well, technically it was. Her command to eat is *essen*."

"Essen? Hmm…I remember Phillip saying all the police dogs are trained to primarily respond to German commands. Is that one?"

"Yes. Though she isn't a police dog, the trainer we worked with trains them too, so he uses German by default." Jessie pulled two jars of pasta sauce out of the pantry as she spoke.

"Ah. I guess that way a crook can't just yell 'sit' at a police dog to stop them."

"Well, that was the basic idea, though they soon realized it was more a matter of training. They are better trained now than the first dogs, so they know not to obey anything said by someone they have been sent after. It's become something of a tradition, though, so it's still done some, though more so with dogs used in the armed forces."

As she poured the sauce into the pan with the hamburger, Galen realized he couldn't see any labels on it and asked what kind it is. "Oh, these are pretty basic pasta sauces, just tomato and a few spices and herbs. I like to keep the jarred ones basic, so I can adjust as needed for recipes."

"Wait, you made those yourself?"

"Yep. I'll make a large batch a few times a year and jar it so it's always on hand."

"Hey dad, Jessie showed me how to make cookies in a jar too," Michael pipped in.

"Cookies, in a jar? Really?" Galen seemed amused at Michael's excitement.

"Yeah, so you can give them as gifts. You put all the dry stuff in the jar in layers, so it looks nice too, then the people you give them to just have to add the eggs and other wet stuff. And the dry batter can last in the jar for a long time!"

"Wow, that sounds fun."

"It is. And you can do it with hot chocolate and cake mix too!"

"I thought hot chocolate came in a little packet in a box with other little packets."

Jessie couldn't help laughing as she finished seasoning the sauce and turning it to simmer. "Well, yes, it can, but real hot chocolate can be made at home easily with just a few ingredients most people already have on hand."

"Hey Jessie, can we make my dad some after dinner? It is so good, Dad, you have to try it!"

"With that kind of recommendation, I'm game if it's alright with you?"

"Of course, nothing finishes off an evening like a cup of hot chocolate, except perhaps some hot chocolate and brownies." Jessie laughed at the excited "yes" that came from both men.

With the sauce simmering, Jessie put together some bowls of salad and joined them at the table. By the time they were done eating, the sauce was ready, so Jessie quickly tossed some spaghetti noodles in a pot of boiling water she'd already had ready on the stove and put the bread in the oven. Ten minutes later, she served everything up.

"Oh my god, this is so good!" Galen said with a moan of appreciation. "It tastes so fresh and has a nice little bit of kick to it."

Jessie blushed at the compliment, knowing it was sincere by the hearty way he was eating. It made her feel warm inside to see him and Michael eating with gusto in her kitchen, even as she ignored the pang of regret over the loss it reminded her of. Tonight was a night for fun, not dwelling on the past or what could never be.

Chapter 20

GALEN AND HIS CREW showed up first thing Monday morning as promised. When the vehicles pulled up, Causy came out to investigate, leaving none of Galen's men inclined to step out of their vehicles at first. Having eaten in the same room with her and knowing her extensive training, Galen was no longer quite as fearful of the dog, so he climbed out of his truck and went to the door to get Jessie. She met him at the screen.

"Good morning," he greeted warmly with a slight wave.

"Good morning. I guess today is the day that it all gets started." She crossed her arms over her chest as if hugging herself.

"Yep, though, my men are a little freaked out by Causy there," Galen said with a chuckle.

Jessie looked over his shoulder to where the big dog stood "at guard" near the steps and quickly called her back to the house. "I'm so sorry. She must've come out while I was in the kitchen making coffee."

With a laugh, Galen told her not to worry about it. "If I catch the guys slacking, I'll just threaten to send her out to visit them."

Jessie chuckled along with him, a sound he was coming to enjoy. Pointing towards the vehicles, she gave Causy two commands. "There, I've told her that they are allowed and to leave them alone. She won't molest them now unless they do something threatening. But I'll keep her in the house, so they won't have to feel afraid."

Speaking of feeling afraid, Galen realized she was trembling. "Anything I can do to make it easier?"

She shook her head, closed her eye, and took a deep breath. Her grip on the door frame tightened for a moment, then she looked back at him. There was still fear in her eye, but more so, there was determination. "It's okay. I'll be okay. I can do this…No, I must do this. But I appreciate the offer."

Galen realized he was getting a little addicted to her smiles. After signaling the men to unload, he reminded her that they would be outside most of the day. "Some of the guys will be going over the siding inch-by-inch to replace loose and broken ones. At the same time, they will check the structure underneath to be sure it's good. Another group will work on the roof, and the third crew will get started on the driveway modifications we talked about."

He suspected it was thanks to the Bradshaw family influence he'd gotten all the necessary building permits within hours of Jessie having signed the contracts. Of course, it rarely took long in town anyway, as they tended to avoid making citizens go through a bunch of red tape, but he'd never gotten any quite that fast. He'd originally planned for Monday to be a prep day, maybe half a day's work, but after receiving the permits, he was able to rearrange it to get renovations fully started. Fortunately, thanks to a small gap in his project schedule, he was able to pull in three crews to really get things going on a good foot.

"That sounds good. Anything you need from me?"

"Not right now. We have a portable bathroom, so you don't have to worry about anyone needing to come into the house. If anything comes up, I'll let you know."

With that, Galen headed off to give his crew their individual instructions, then rotated between them to supervise the work and lend a hand whenever needed.

Jessie returned to the house to spend the day working, easily tuning out the construction noise. She also kept the blinds in the office closed, so she wouldn't see the shadows of the men moving around outside.

Near lunch, she heard a ferocious series of barks and snarls just as Causy jumped up and headed towards the front door. Moments later a man's terrified cry added extra speed to Jessie's feet as she followed the dog. Galen was right behind her as they ran to Thor's kennel. One of the men was near the door, several wooden boards scattered around him while the man himself was looking at the raging dog in horror.

"Are you alright?" Galen asked as he helped the man up.

"Yes, sir, I am, I just. I'm sorry ma'am, I didn't mean to set him off. Didn't even see him in there, then he just came at me." The man stammered, warily glancing between the dog and Jessie. No doubt he thought he might be in trouble, though he'd done nothing wrong.

"It's okay. I'm so sorry he scared you like that. He's been unwell." Turning to Thor, Jessie commanded him to be quiet, and told him he was acting badly. Thor continued to rage at the man, ignoring her completely.

"Come on," Galen said, helping the man pick up the wood before leading him towards the house again. "He should calm down once we're out of his territory," he said, giving Jessie a questioning look.

"Yes, he should. Again, I'm sorry."

Jessie stayed with Thor, occasionally commanding him again to be quiet. After several long minutes, he finally put his feet back on the ground and obeyed, his attention now on her. He stood tense, as usual, not tilting his head to question what the next command was, but still he pressed himself against the door, as if seeking reassurance.

She squatted down in front of the door and pushed her fingers through the wire to give his fur a few strokes. "Oh,

Thor. I know you're still in there somewhere. You gotta fight the fear boy, don't let it eat you."

When she returned to her office, Galen was waiting. "Is that man okay?"

"Yeah, shook up a bit, but he'll be alright." He looked at her in concern. "How about you? You doing okay?"

Though she was still shaking from the adrenalin running through her, she nodded. "Startled me, for sure, but I'll be okay. Please, let him know I'm sorry."

"Don't worry, he knows it wasn't your fault or anything. I warned the other men to stick to the right side of the house if they need to bring anything from the front again, rather than risk going near Thor's kennel."

"Good idea. I should have thought of that before." Jessie tried to think of something else to say but caught herself before she tried to extend the conversation just to keep him near for a little longer. "I should let you get back to work."

"Alrighty. I'll be outside if you need me." He nodded to her and headed back outside. Jessie forced herself to return to her office and her own work, though it took several starts and stops before she stopped having fantasy conversations with Galen in her head.

Once she was back in her groove, she was able to work without interruption until Galen popped in just before five to let her know they were packing up for the day.

The same pattern repeated for most of the week, with Jessie's work only interrupted slightly on the day they did the window replacements. Galen came inside to do all the covering of floors and cutting there himself, so Jessie didn't have to deal with a stranger in the house just yet.

By Friday, the house was both a mess and yet already improved with its freshly painted exterior, new windows, and new bright red door. The framing was in place for the bathroom expansion and the wires to power the planned lights and ceiling fans being added to the wrap-around porch were also installed. She loved her new paved driveway curving in front of the house, allowing room for two vehicles to be side by side and to accommodate parking for guests.

After the crew left, Galen stopped in to say goodnight and let her know what had gotten done, just as he'd done each night of the week. When they were done reviewing the renovations, Jessie asked if he had any plans for the weekend.

"Nothing too big. Mostly just hanging around the house, doing chores, things like that. Why, is something up?"

"Well, um, I don't know if you knew, but my friend Jazza owns Razzmatazz in town?"

"Oh, yeah, I knew she owned, but it wasn't until just now that it clicked she was the same Jazza. You'd think it would have been obvious from the name, not exactly common." He grinned in self-deprecation.

"It's okay, don't we all have moments like that?" Jessie joked back. "Well, I mentioned it because, well tomorrow she's closing the restaurant for a few hours to do a tasting party. Basically trying a bunch of new dishes she is considering adding to the menu. It will be my first big outing besides the store, and I thought maybe you and Michael might like to join us?"

"Is it going to be a big crowd?" He asked, worried it might be too big a jump for her to make. The store was mostly ignoring strangers, but this sounded like a more personal event.

She shook her head. "Just my brothers and Silky Aria. Julianna won't be there, as she had to go out of town this weekend. And well, you two if you decide you want to come."

Galen smiled. "Good food and joining a friend in a big achievement? Yeah, I think we can arrange that. Want to ride in to town together?"

Warmth spread through Jessie at his smile and his acceptance. In truth, it had taken her all week to work up the nerve to ask, even knowing the longer she waited the more likely it would become they had plans. "That sounds great. Pick me up around 2:45?"

"Will do. See you tomorrow." Galen found himself whistling his way back to his truck. Once he was behind the wheel, he caught sight of his face in the rearview mirror. "Quit grinning, you idiot, this is not a date. Just friends hanging out at a local event, that's all."

He was still telling himself that when they pulled up in front of Jessie's house the next day, right up until Jessie stepped out on the porch in a pair of blue jeans that fit her far too well and a long-sleeved, high-neck pale yellow blouse that hugged her curves perfectly. He hated watching those curves disappear under her jacket as she came down the stairs.

"You look nice." He told her as she got into the car beside him.

Jessie looked at him in surprise, then blushed before turning her attention to fastening the seat belt. "Oh, um, thank you."

"Hey Jessie, how are you doing?" Michael asked from the backseat.

"Not too bad. Pretty hungry though, how about you?" Jessie replied, turning in her seat to look at him behind Galen.

"Yeah, me too. We decided not to eat too much breakfast, so we could have room for all the food this afternoon. We've had dinner at Razzmatazz before and it was really good."

"Definitely one of my favorite places in town and I'm not just saying that to get a friend hookup," Galen added with a wink, happy to see no signs of shaking or fear today.

Even if it was just a family event, he was proud of her for facing her fear of being in public to go. He also thought she'd done great dealing with the men being around the house. By the end of the weak, she was barely shaking at all when they arrived in the morning and started unloading. He hoped it was a good sign, considering the step he was planning to ask her to make next.

Chapter 21

As they entered the restaurant, Silky Aria rushed over to embrace Jessie tight, tears shining in her eyes. "I've missed you so much!"

Returning the hug Jessie felt a twinge of guilt for not having called her since returning to town. Jessie and two of the Aria sisters had met in high school and become fast friends. As such, they were considered part of the Bradshaw family.

The Aria family had been one of the first to inhabit the town, and each generation had elected to stay on including at least part of the current. Silky still lived in town, as did the younger sister Roxy, when she wasn't off conducting investigations for the PI firm she worked for. Only Kat had completely left, moving out to California after graduating high school and not returning.

Silky tended to be very conscientious of other people's wishes so while she may have wanted to call or visit many times, she wouldn't have done so if she thought Jessie wouldn't be okay with it. "I'm sorry, I should've called before now. I've been hiding way too long."

"It's okay, I understand. After the accident, Kat was the same way at first. I knew I'd get to see you when you were ready and here you are!" Silky replied with a smile.

Jessie introduced her to Galen and Michael. As they joined the others, Silky chatted with Michael and learned he'd be starting middle school next year. Silky told him she was looking forward to seeing him in her class, as she taught middle school English.

Leaving them to talk about what middle school would be like, Jessie led Galen over to where her brothers stood near the middle of the room. From the moment they had walked in, Galen had felt their gaze on him. It occurred to him that from an outside perspective, Jessie bringing him and Michael to the event could be interpreted as her introducing a potential significant other to the family. It would certainly explain the assessing glares of the three Bradshaw men as they made their way to them.

"Hey guys, you probably already know him, but this Galen Andrews. And that adorable boy talking to Silky is his son Michael." Jessie introduced him with a smile. "Galen, these are my brothers, Julian, Jack, and James. And before you ask, yes, Dad was the one who convinced our mom that we all had to have names starting with J. It was a family thing."

Chuckling, Galen faced Julian first. He knew the other man casually, having met him through Phillip and seeing him around town on patrol. A quiet man, he greeted Galen with a warm handshake. "Welcome, glad you could make it."

Likewise, Galen had met Jack once or twice. He'd come to welcome Galen and Michael to town personally, apparently one of the many things he did as part of his duties to the town. He radiated friendliness, giving Galen a hearty handshake and a wide grin. "Good to see you again. Really excited to see how the work is coming along with the house. I know you'll do her right."

James was the one Galen had never met or could remember seeing in town. "Good of you to join us." While his words were outwardly friendly, Galen felt an irrational fear of Jessie's oldest brother. He realized now why his teenaged friends, who'd frequently talked about their crushes on the Bradshaw girls, had never had the nerve to ask them on a date. With his dark features and coldly assessing glare, he reminded Galen of a movie that featured a polite, quiet, but chilling Death in human form. Mentally shaking the image from his head, Galen nevertheless knew—without any words spoken beyond that polite greeting—if he ever did anything to hurt Jessie, he'd have to answer to this man and would likely come out the loser.

In the next moment, the cold façade faded as James hugged Jessie tight and kissed her cheek. "Hey, Lil' Bit. Glad you could make it."

James held Jessie's hand as they made their way to the table, leaving Galen mildly amused at the obvious hint. He might be her "date," but she was still the much beloved baby sister and family came first. Still, Galen couldn't find it in himself to be insulted, he'd have probably been just as protective of his baby sister if he'd had one.

Rather than the usual seating, the tables in the restaurant had been rearranged to make one long table so they could all sit together. Michael sat between Jessie and Galen, while Jack, Julian, and Silky sat across from them. James, of course, sat at the head of the table, with Jazza at the other end.

All in all, they tried a dozen dishes served by two of Jazza's wait staff. After each dish, Jazza had them fill out feedback cards to rate the qualities of the dish and note what they liked and didn't like. Even Michael was allowed to offer his feedback. Galen was proud his son had gamely tried every dish, even if he looked at one or two with a raised eyebrow.

During the drive back to Jessie's house, they chatted about all the food they'd tried. With the driveway still curing, Galen drove alongside it and parked nearby, then got out to walk Jessie to the door. He told himself he just wanted to make sure she made it back okay over the uneven ground. Standing with her at her door while she was still flushed with happiness over the evening, Galen swallowed hard and his mouth was moving before he could really think about what he was saying.

"I know this might be sudden, but I was wondering if you'd like to have dinner with me sometime."

"Sure, I mean, we've had dinner together a few times now." Jessie looked at him with a confused expression.

"Well, I was thinking more of just us two, as in a, um, date."

"Oh." Her eyes widened in surprise and Galen worried he'd scared her. "You, you really want to go on a date with…me? Why would you want to go on a date with me?"

He'd started to think she was as curious about him as he was about her, but maybe he'd been wrong. Still, he'd already put his foot in it so might as well finish it up. "Usual reasons I guess. I find you interesting and attractive. We're both single so it seemed like the next logical step to exploring that interest."

"You find me attractive?" Doubt and confusion colored her voice.

Worried he'd pushed her too far, Galen decided to let it drop for tonight. "Yes, very much so, but you don't have to answer now. Just, well…maybe think about it?" With that, he turned to walk back down the stairs, but her light touch on his arm stopped him.

"Okay. Yes. I'd…I'd like that." Though it wasn't the most enthusiastic of yeses, it and the shaky smile still made it a yes! Grinning like a kid who'd found the cookie jar, Galen asked her if Friday evening would work for her and she agreed. Promising to pick her up at seven, Galen nearly danced back to the car. As he climbed in, James' stern face flashed through his mind. Had he just pulled the tiger's tail?

$$Chapter\ 22$$

BY THE END OF THE following week, the porch was done and some of the crew had moved inside to complete work on the balcony, as well as start the bedroom and bathroom renovations. The first day they came in was the hardest. Every sound they made had Jessie twitching, even though it wasn't that much louder than the work outside had been. Just knowing it was coming from inside the house was enough to make it worse to her mind.

Anytime she came out of her office to refill her drink or go to the bathroom, she'd jump if she spotted one of the men. It left her nerves constantly on edge and by the end of the day she was exhausted from it all. The weak part of her wanted to call it off, to beg Galen to save the inside work for another time, but she refused to give in. Instead, she focused her attention on relocating her sleeping quarters to the living room and moving her clothes to the office closets so the men could work in the bedroom.

The second day, it was if her flight or fight response system had burnt out from being so reactive, leaving her relatively calm and far less jumpy. It gave her more time to question the wisdom of accepting Galen's date. Part of her was excited, looking forward to her first date in a long time, but she was also terrified that something would happen. They'd be asked to leave because of her appearance or that flashbacks would ruin the evening.

Hoping it wasn't against some unknown dating rule, she checked with Galen to find out where they were going. He had reservations for them at Five Fifty Three in Sylva, a nice restaurant that was relatively expensive. A quick check of her closet confirmed what she'd already known: she had absolutely nothing fancier to wear. Her nicest outfits were, at best, business casual, and there wasn't a dress to be seen.

Though she was shaking at the thought of it, she called Jazza for an emergency shopping trip. Jazza swung by an hour later to pick her up, and after some indecision, they decided to go to the historic Grove Arcade in Asheville, and possibly Biltmore Park if Jessie was up to it.

"To be honest, I am so freaking terrified right now," she told Jazza as they made the long drive to the shopping center.

Jessie tried to stop herself from continually clenching her fists and to keep her breathing under control.

"I know. You're pale as a ghost. If it gets to be too much, just say the word and we can leave. Even trying is a huge step," Jazza told her with a concerned look.

"Thanks, I'm going to give it my best shot."

"Would it help if we'd brought along a certain adorable cherub to hold your hand?"

Jessie laughed. "He is adorable, isn't he? And maybe. Though he'd probably be pretty bored shopping for women's clothes."

"I'm amazed you said yes to the date."

"Me too. I'm still not sure if it was me or someone just jumped in my body to say yes."

"If it was, smart lady," Jazza said with a chuckle. "Galen is a good man, and it seems like he and his little boy have been good for you so far."

"Yeah. He was very kind about my being afraid of him, even though it had to bother him on some level. No one would want someone to be afraid of them for seemingly no reason. And he's been wonderful about the house renovation, helping ease me into the men being in the house. I don't think I'm afraid of him anymore."

"Well, I'd hope not if you're going to have a fun date." Jazza winked at her. "Now, the big question is: are you attracted to him in a platonic fashion or…?"

Jessie sighed. "I'm not sure. It's…it's hard for me to imagine being intimate with a man. Even the thought triggers flashbacks. And I have a hard time imagining any man wanting me physically. While Galen said he finds me attractive, he hasn't really seen any of my scars yet."

"With the way he looked at you the other day, I'd say he definitely wants you. Now, if he runs after seeing the scars, then he never deserved you anyway. But I don't think he will. He is a strong-hearted man. You know he stayed devoted to his wife while she was dying from cancer and hasn't dated since she passed on. So, if it helps, it's the first date in a long time for both of you."

"Really? He hasn't dated at all!?" Jessie found it hard to believe a man who looked as good as Galen hadn't gone on even a casual date in the three years since his wife had passed.

"Nope, not a one. Not for lack of offers either. I guess he's mostly be focused on raising that sweet little boy of his."

"He is a sweetheart, and I've loved having him visit. To be honest, it worries me a little."

"Why?"

"I can't help worrying if my attraction to Galen has more to do with Michael since I can't have children of my own." Jessie's voice caught as she remembered the doctor coming in to apologize and explain that her insides were so badly damaged that a hysterectomy was required. Jazza had been there with James, each holding one of her hands as the doctor gave her the painful news. And they'd both held her as she'd cried. She'd always dreamed of having children someday.

"It could be. They are a package deal after all. But I think if that was all it was, you'd have to really be pushing yourself to be excited about this date and you wouldn't be as worried about what he'll think of you." Jazza grinned. "If nothing else, I bet Michael is turning cartwheels right now over you two going on a date."

"Really? You don't think he might think I'm trying to replace his mom or something?"

"Nope, he's a smart kid and no doubt Galen will explain dating to him, to some degree, just to be safe. Besides, at the tasting, he confided in me that he hoped his dad likes you."

In Asheville, Jazza held Jessie's hand for the start of their shopping trip. By the third store, Jessie was doing okay without it, as long as Jazza stayed nearby. Jessie managed to find a dress and matching shoes, and at Jazza's urging, a few more new outfits for future outings and for the upcoming Thanksgiving dinner. As a trial run, they even ate lunch at a mall restaurant. The waitress gave Jessie's glasses a double-take but didn't say anything more and was still as friendly and cheerful as when she first walked up to the table. A few patrons glanced their way, but overall, they had a pleasant lunch.

It was evening when they returned to Jessie's house. Before they parted company, Jazza hugged her tight. "You go, enjoy yourself. No better way to show him that he didn't win than by not being afraid to be happy, okay?"

"I know…and he hasn't won, not yet."

"Damn right."

Chapter 23

GALEN HADN'T BEEN SO nervous since Michael learned to walk and fall. He stood at Jessie's door right at seven, asking himself yet again if he was sure he knew what he was doing. When she opened the door, his doubts vanished in awe as she stood there in a gray sheath that flowed down her body and rested just above her ankles. A black long-sleeved jacket covered her arms. It wasn't super fancy, but on her it was amazingly elegant and flattering. The gray really enhanced her visible eye and the dress itself tastefully enhanced all her wonderful feminine curves.

"You look amazing." His nearly whispered comment earned him a smile, a blush, and a murmured thank you. He liked that she was ready, her slim black purse and keys in hand, rather than making him wait while she did final touch-ups.

Returning the smile, he held out his hand and led her to the truck. On the way to Sylva, they chatted amicably about the house renovations and Galen's work in general. Jessie enjoyed hearing about the projects he'd worked on, especially the historical renovations. His love of his work was obvious in the enthusiastic way he talked about it.

When she saw him working at her house, he was usually dressed in jeans and a t-shirt or simple pullover that left her staring at his well-muscled arms and chest. Tonight, those long legs were encased in black trousers, while his lovely muscles were just barely hidden in a well-tailored white dress shirt and a black jacket. She had to agree with Jazza's earlier assessment; he was indeed hunky.

From the way the hostess at the restaurant eyed him as they were being seated, she wasn't the only one who noticed. In a way, it didn't bother her, as it kept the woman from staring at her. They were led to a nice private table and Jessie was touched by Galen's thoughtfulness in making such a reservation. After placing their wine and appetizer orders, Galen turned the conversation to her.

"So, I know now that Mr. Clark considered you a granddaughter, but I was wondering how that happened? I mean, y'all weren't related by blood at all, right?"

"Right...I guess you could say it was one of those rare moments when fate decides to throw you a bone. When we moved here, I'd wandered away from the house and got lost in the woods. Grandpa was out in the same area, shooting wildlife with his camera and he found me, led me home. He was so nice that afterward, I went to thank him. Learning he had no family, I guess I felt kinship with him, so I started visiting him and eventually he became a member of the family."

"He was a great old guy…loved kids, it was plain to see, even though he never had any of his own."

"That was always so sad to me because I think he'd have been a great father."

The waitress interrupted to deliver their crabbed stuffed mushrooms and took their dinner orders.

"You mentioned moving here? I thought the Bradshaws had been here forever?"

With a laugh, Jessie confirmed they usually were. "In our case though, my mom and I lived in Carrboro instead of here. I think it was to be closer to my siblings at the time since Julian and Julianna were attending the School of Science and Math, and Jack and James were both at Carolina. After she died, James moved us back here, though Julian and Julianna did go to college out of town once we were resettled."

"So, you've been here most of your life?"

"Yes. Mom died on my tenth birthday, and James moved us here not long after."

"Oh, wow, that must make birthdays hard?"

"It used to. I know she died in a car accident with Jazza's parents, and I can remember not liking my birthday for a while after, but with Jazza and my siblings, I moved past it. I was so young at the time, I…sometimes, I barely remember. It's hard for me to really remember what Mom looked like. I can only rely on pictures my brother gave me. But I can remember her singing me to sleep at night and holding my hand, walking through the park. Little snippets like that. I don't really remember the day she died at all, though from what James told me later, I was pretty shocked, so that's probably why I've forgotten."

"In some ways, Michael is the same. He was only seven when cancer took Melinda away, so I show him pictures and tell him stories, hoping it helps him know her, but not sure if he really feels like he does."

"I think he does." Jessie hesitated for a moment before adding, "We, um, we ran into each other at the cemetery once. He was there to visit her, and I was there to visit Grandpa's grave. He introduced me to her, and I could tell he really loved his mom."

"She was a good mom, so I know she'd be glad he still remembers her. She was diagnosed three years before she died, and we kind of always knew it was coming. She tried to prepare us as best she could. She wrote him letters for me to give him at certain ages and made him a scrapbook of memories to help him remember her."

"I'm sure he'll treasure them, especially as he gets older."

The waitress returned with their dinner, and the conversation turned to the dishes they had ordered. Jessie loved the spicy shrimp and grits, which were topped with a wonderful

Creole-style gravy. Sharing Jessie's love of spicy food, Galen had opted for the seafood diablo, which featured shrimp, clams, and mussels tossed with fresh vegetables in a hot marinara sauce. They ended up sampling each other's dishes as well, sharing as easily as they might have with their respective families.

"So, you moved Michael here after Melinda passed?"

"Yep. It was hard living in that house and I felt like we needed a change to help us bounce back. You already know we used to visit here as kids, and it wasn't a place I ever forgot. Phillip had already moved here a few years before to work for the police force. He gave me the idea and once he mentioned it, I knew it was what we needed."

"Was it difficult to restart your business here?"

"In some ways, but the local business association was a lot of help, and I came with some good, solid references from my early work in Cary. Your brother, Jack, helped as well by hiring me to do the renovation of the library. That gained me more local attention."

"Really? I didn't know about that, though it doesn't surprise me. He and James take their duty to the town seriously, including wanting to help newcomers have a chance to make a good life. He's helped folks who come to town find jobs, homes, etc. We want them to know we take care of our own, you know, and we consider you our own if you live here."

"It is a great thing and certainly a sure way to ensure newcomers feel both welcomed and like they made the right choice in coming here. I have heard about Jack doing quite a bit regarding city management and stuff but didn't realize James does as well."

"He tends work in the background, taking care of the big issues and handling a lot of the financial stuff, ensuring the town has plenty of cash to keep the city services going, things like that."

"I guess it's a full-time job for both of them, even with a town our size?"

"Oh, it can be, but James also works as a security consultant. He travels around the world helping individuals, companies, etc. with setting up security systems or improving them. Jack works with him in that as well, sometimes traveling with him, sometimes working on his own."

"Ah…you know, now that I think about it, he is out of town a lot, isn't he? I hadn't really thought about it before. I guess it must be nice, traveling so much and seeing all kinds of places."

"He seems to enjoy it, and he always brings Jazza and me all kinds of interesting and unusual souvenirs. Even now, he just came back from a trip to Japan and brought me a beautiful handmade kimono."

"I bet you'd look really pretty in a kimono."

Jessie's heart skipped a beat at his flirtatious grin. "I, um, I wore one as a girl once or twice, but not as an adult. Maybe I'll, ah, give it a try one day and you can tell me how I look."

"I can't wait."   Another sexy smile, another skipped heartbeat.

After dinner, they were both easily tempted into lingering over cups of coffee and a shared piece of decadent chocolate cake. They talked about their hobbies and were amused to find they shared a love of B-rated natural horror films, particularly snake and shark flicks. On the drive back to Cascade Falls, they continued talking about their tastes in films and books and enjoyed a lively discussion on books adapted into films—which were well done, and which not so much.

Back at her house, Galen walked her to the door, holding her hand as they went up the steps. Jessie unlocked the door but didn't go in just yet, wanting a few more moments with him.

"I had a wonderful time tonight, I truly did. Thank you."

"No, thank you, because I did too. I'd love to do it again, if you'd like?"

"I'd really like that," she replied with a smile.

"I, um, I'd really like to kiss you right now, but I don't want to scare you."

Jessie decided he looked so cute when he was unsure of himself, then realized what he was saying. Slowly, hesitantly, she touched his chin and took a deep breath.

"I'd like to try it, if you don't mind?"

Galen's eyes went wide for a moment before he slowly lowered his head, giving her plenty of time to back out if she wanted. Closing her eyes, Jessie said a quick prayer that her fears would stay away; then as his clean, crisp scent tickled her nose, she stopped thinking altogether. His lips softly brushed against hers in a near feather-light kiss, a gentle hello with no pressure or demands. Despite the casualness, she still had a brief flashback that sent a tell-tale tremble through her hand, but then it was gone, buried beneath the tingling warmth radiating from that single brief touch throughout her body.

He pulled back, a smile decorating those same soft lips as his hand caressed her cheek. "We definitely need to do that again sometime." He leaned forward and kissed her forehead before letting her go. With a whispered "good night," he headed back to his truck.

Jessie stood on the porch and watched his taillights go down the street to his own house. Finally, she went back inside where an anxious Causy awaited. After closing the door, she leaned back against it and brought her fingers up to her lips, the lips his had just kissed. He'd kissed her…and she'd kissed him…and it had been wonderful.

Patting Causy, she hummed to herself as she headed into the house to get settled for the night.

Chapter 24

THE NEXT MORNING, Jazza dropped by to talk about Jessie's date over breakfast. After all their years of friendship, Jessie had expected her enough to prep the ingredients to make French toast and put on a pot of water to boil for grits. Jazza followed her into the kitchen and hit the fridge to pull out bacon. They worked together amicably, long used to cooking together. After their parents' deaths, Jessie and Jazza had both wanted to help around the house, and as Jessie's mom had already started teaching her the basics of cooking, they decided that would be their job. Fortunately, they'd learned quickly, with help from Julianna.

It took Jazza ten minutes to break. "Okay girl, stop leaving me in suspense! Did you have fun?"

Chuckling, Jessie debated not answering yet just to torment her a little more, but she was too happy not to share. "It was more wonderful than I could have imagined. He was polite and attentive, and I loved talking to him. I can't remember the last time I had such a great time on a date."

"I sense sparks here?"

"I think so…I really want to believe so, but I'm scared too. He wants to go on a date again, I think, at least he sounded like he wanted to, and he said he enjoyed it."

"Well, if you both had a good time, I'd say he probably does."

"I know, I just…I feel like, if we're going to keep doing this, dating and maybe trying to have a relationship, I should tell him what happened. I enjoyed him kissing me, but it was light and simple. If he wants to do more, and I start freaking out on him, he should at least know why, right?"

"I can understand what you're thinking, and I think you're probably right. But, do you feel like you're ready?"

Jessie understood her concerns. She'd never really talked about the details of what had happened to anyone, not her family, not Jazza, not the hospital psychiatrist. With the police, it had been "just the facts." She knew her family had likely read the police reports, so they understood the basics, but the way she felt, the real details, she'd refused to speak about and tried to avoid thinking about it. To tell Galen would mean deliberately returning to the living nightmare and reliving it.

"It absolutely terrifies me. But I don't want either of us wasting our time or risking our hearts, if he can't come to terms with what happened or can't handle knowing about it."

"Gotcha, so when do you think you will?"

"I'm not sure. I guess first we see if he even asks me out on another date."

"Ha, I bet he calls you before the end of the weekend!"

They moved to the kitchen table to eat their breakfast. Moving to a lighter topic, they discussed the menu for Thanksgiving dinner. The Bradshaw family dined at the restaurant every year, rather than any particular house. It had the biggest kitchen and plenty of room. Jazza closed the restaurant for the holidays, and the family took over the building to cook the meal and to eat.

In addition to the Bradshaws themselves, including Jazza of course, they always invited anyone who didn't have someone to spend the holidays with. Several locals who had no family and didn't want to impose on friends attended each year, with the restaurant locale making them feel less like they were a burden. This year, Jazza and Jessie would be taking care of the main menu, with several of their regular diners bringing potluck dishes.

"I've already picked up a turkey and a ham, both enormous. I'm thinking for their size, we better get started sometime Wednesday so they can be finished in time."

"Agreed. For the turkey this year, I was thinking about trying a basting sauce made with some Johnny Walker black label."

Jazza moaned appreciatively. "Oh, I bet that will be good. You always make such yummy drunk turkeys." They shared a laugh over the shared memory of a 16-year-old Jessie horrifying her poor brothers by making their Thanksgiving turkey and using some of Jack's twenty-three-year-old bourbon. All her brothers had an appreciation for expensive alcohol, and they couldn't believe she'd used a cup of the $1,000 whiskey. Still, they had all agreed, it was a very tasty turkey.

"For sides, I can take care of the macaroni and cheese, candied yams, cabbage, stuffing, and the mashed potatoes."

"Great! I'll take care of the ham, green bean casserole, corn, potato salad, deviled eggs, oh, and an orange-cranberry sauce to go with that turkey. Will you make those super buttery crescent rolls?"

"Of course. I think my brothers would throw a tantrum if I didn't."

"Ha, they wouldn't be the only ones! Now, let's think dessert."

"Hmm, mile-high apple pie, banana pudding, rum cake?"

"Sweet potato pie and maybe a French silk pie? Man, I'm getting hungry again!"

"Me too!"

With the menu set, they agreed to meet at the restaurant Wednesday morning, so they would have time to get everything going. They would stay there most of that day and night, with the Bradshaw men stopping by to bring them lunch and dinner, as well as breakfast on Thanksgiving Day.

After Jazza left, Jessie wondered what Galen and Michael would be doing for Thanksgiving. She debated calling and asking if they'd like to join them, but remembering Galen's brother was also in town, she figured they would probably spend the day together.

Confirming Jazza's theory, Galen called her Sunday evening to chat and ask her if she'd like to go out again on Saturday. Of course, she told him she'd love to, and they agreed he'd pick her up at the same time.

"Oh, by the way, with the holidays, the crew will only be out on Monday and Tuesday. I meant to tell you Friday but was so excited, I forgot."

"That sounds fine to me. You're a nice boss to let your guys off on Wednesday and Friday too."

"Yeah, a lot of them have families and I'd rather they be home helping their wives get ready and dealing with company than worrying about it while trying to work."

Spotting the opening, Jessie tried to be casual as she asked how he'd be spending the holiday.

"Well, neither Phillip nor I have the skills to do much in the kitchen with regards to real Thanksgiving food, so we'll probably just go out to eat like we usually do each year."

"Oh, well, um, you know, we have dinner over at Razzmatazz each year for the family and anyone in town who might otherwise spend the day alone. Jazza and I are making tons of food. You guys would be more than welcome to join us."

"Yeah, I think I remember Jack mentioning that when we first moved here. Don't know why I never considered it before." Dropping his voice lower, Galen teased her. "Would I get to see you looking so good in another one of those sexy dresses?"

Jessie felt her checks flush and surprised herself by giving in to the urge to flirt back. "Mmm, that might be a possibility, though I guess you'd have to be the judge of whether it's sexy or not." Galen groaned in response, making her giggle. "So is that a yes?"

"Let's see. Good food, especially food made by you and getting to spend the day with you in what I'm now certain will be a sexy dress, I can't see any negatives here."

Still in the grips of the return of her bolder, pre-terrified self, Jessie stage-whispered, "If you're really good, you might even get to steal another kiss, or two."

"We're there!"

Jessie fell back in her chair laughing. God, it felt so good to flirt and tease him as a normal woman might do with an attractive guy. "Great. We do it kind of brunch style, so come on by around 2 or so."

"I'll see you then, except when seeing you in my dreams." Jessie knew if anyone saw her now, she'd be blushing as she hung up the phone.

Chapter 25

WORK CONTINUED ON the house on Monday and Tuesday as promised. During the crew's lunch break, Galen found Jessie to spend the time with her, feeling something like a high schooler again, wanting to be with his new girl all the time. Galen wondered if it was too soon to think of her as "his girl." It would probably seem strange to some people, but their first date had helped him realize Jessie had become special to him and he wasn't one for just doing some kind of casual fling. He hoped it wasn't a one-sided desire.

Knowing her as he did, he didn't think this was likely a casual for her either, particularly given her initial fears of him and of people in general. Would she tell him what had really happened in Chicago? Eventually, he knew they needed to talk about it, particularly if they decided to really get serious with things, but for now, he was content to just enjoy their fledgling relationship and the fun of getting to know each other more.

With her spending the day at the restaurant with Jazza on Wednesday, Galen offered to do one of the meal drop-offs for the girls. He almost expected her brothers to protest but was happy when he received a call asking him if he could pick up their dinner order from a local Chinese restaurant and bring it by.

He stayed with them while they ate and peeked around the kitchen to see how they were doing. Initially, he was concerned about them being alone all night, but they reassured him that James would be coming by later to stay with them and the doors would all be locked. While the town wasn't a hotbed of crime, there was no sense in inviting trouble. He could tell they were both tired but enjoying the tradition of preparing meals for their family and friends. Before heading home, he followed up on his promise to steal another sweet kiss when Jessie walked him to the door.

During the night, the women continued cooking with James alternately helping with any lifting and the like and dozing in one of the restaurant booths. At one point, after putting the turkey back in the oven for Jessie, James lingered in the kitchen while Jazza took a bathroom break.

"So, I heard Galen and his son are joining us?"

"Oh, yeah, and Galen's brother too. They were going to eat out anyway, and, um…" Jessie trailed off, not sure how to bring up the fact that she and Galen were dating. Jazza would have told him, of course, but still, that was different from telling herself. It made her feel almost like she was in a confessional.

James smiled and kissed her forehead. "It's okay. I already figured it was something special for you to go on a date with him, so I wasn't that surprised. He seems like good people, so I won't go scaring him, yet." He teased. "As long as you're happy, that's what matters to me."

"I am, I think. He makes me feel alive again, you know, but at the same time it's scary." Jessie replied, folding her arms across her chest to chase away the sudden chill. "It feels almost too fast and like it's too good to be true, you know? I keep feeling like I'm going to wake up from a dream any minute."

"It's only natural. It's your first time dating in a long time and it hasn't been that long since you've been home. I know it probably won't help to say try not to worry, but still, try not to. It's good to see you smile so much again." James gave her a hug. "Even if it doesn't work out in the end, I think he and Michael did a lot to help you recover, so I'm grateful to them for that. And for what it's worth, I'm rooting for you two."

Jessie smiled and hugged him tight. While she would do what she wanted either way, it meant a lot to her to know James supported them.

In the morning, Jack brought by breakfast. Slightly better in the kitchen than James, Jazza and James eventually left him there to keep an eye on the food while they returned to their respective homes to change and for Jessie to feed Thor his breakfast and spend a little time with him. The holidays had interrupted their usual schedule, and she didn't want to lose the scant progress they had made

Jessie was humming in the car as she thought about the coming day. As her house came into sight, her happiness was replaced with curiosity then unmitigated terror at the sight of a strange car in her driveway. Who was at her house and why? Could Crichton have escaped? She was shaking so badly she had to hold the steering wheel in a death grip to maintain control.

Continuing past the house, she finally let go of the wheel with one hand long enough to reach for her cell phone, but it wasn't there. Cursing, she realized it was sitting on the counter at the restaurant. Instead, she pulled into Galen's drive as if it had been her destination. Taking some deep breaths, she walked quickly up to the door, trying not to run in case the person at her house was watching.

"Hey, Jessie, is something wrong?" Michael frowned up at her after answering her knock. Jessie forced herself to smile.

"Nothing too bad, honey. Is your dad home?"

"Yeah, come on in." As she entered the house, Michael turned and yelled for his dad. When Galen came down the stairs, he took one look at Jessie and asked Michael to go back upstairs and finish getting ready for lunch. With a concerned look at Jessie, Michael obeyed.

"What's wrong, sweetheart?" Galen came and took her hands in his.

"There's someone parked outside my house. I don't know who. I've never seen that car before."

"What?" Cautiously, Galen went to the side window and eased the curtain to the side.

"Can I use your phone to call my brother?"

"Of course. I can call Phillip too."

"No, it's okay, he's off today, right? I'll just call James." Galen looked at her curiously and she knew he wondered why she'd rather call her oldest brother over the police. Especially when one of her brothers was a police officer. Apparently, he decided not to ask as he handed her the phone without question. Her conversation with James was short. As soon as she told him what was happening, he said he'd be there in ten minutes and hung up. It only took him five and Jack was with him. They came to Galen's and after checking on Jessie, they went out Galen's back door.

Watching them, Galen found himself understanding how they would be good security guys. Their faces serious, eyes cold, he'd be damned scared of trying to come after someone or something they were guarding. He wondered why they went out the back and tried to watch from inside the house, but it was like they had vanished. He held Jessie's hand and tried to help her stay calm while they waited.

After fifteen minutes, James called Galen's house phone and told Jessie it was okay to come back to her house. Galen wanted to go with her, but Jessie asked him to please wait there, reassuring him that she'd be okay. Standing on his front porch, he hated watching her get in the car and drive up to her house without him, without knowing who was there or what was going on. If Michael hadn't been upstairs, he never would have willingly stayed behind to wait for word on what was going on.

Pulling into her drive, Jessie still tried fathoming what her brother had said, that her unknown visitor was Special Agent Richards. What on earth could he want, and on Thanksgiving Day at that? She went inside where Jack waited by the door.

"He's in the living room, but you don't have to talk to him if you don't want to."

"Why is he here?"

"He said he just wanted to check in on you, see how you were doing. When he got here and found you weren't home, he wasn't sure what to do. I have the feeling he came down here at the last minute, maybe without even realizing what he was doing at first."

Nodding, Jessie walked to the living room door, Jack right behind her. Richards sat on her couch, his head buried in his hands. Seeing her there, James came over to see what she wanted to do. She had no reason to fear he was there to hurt her and could only wonder what would have brought him there unannounced. He was perhaps the only person who had a truly inkling of what how hellish her nightmare had been. Assuring James she was okay, she asked her brothers to leave her alone to talk to Richards. After one more glance at the man on the touch, they headed to the kitchen.

"Agent Richards?" He looked up as she approached, and she couldn't help but pity him. The first time she'd met him, he'd been a sharp dressed, sharp-eyed agent, with his blond hair slicked back. He'd been a little cocky, but better mannered than most agents. She'd researched him before meeting, of course, and knew he became a Special Agent at an unusually young age and was a damn good investigator, top of his game.

Only a shadow of that man sat on her couch, his clothes ill-fitting, hair disheveled, eyes reflecting both tiredness and a strange wildness that concerned her. Sitting beside him, she asked if he was okay, but he didn't seem to hear her.

"Jessie. I'm sorry, I'm sorry…I didn't think, I didn't mean to startle you like this."

"It's alright, no harm done," Jessie spoke to him softly, feeling the urge to comfort him somehow, though she wasn't sure how. "What brings you by? I would've thought you'd spend this day with your family. Your mom is in Georgia, right?"

"Hmm? This day?"

"Yes, Thanksgiving?"

"Oh, is it Thanksgiving already? I hadn't even noticed. I'm sorry, I'm probably disturbing y'all. I'd imagine you were with your family." He looked as if he might run and Jessie's instincts screamed at her not to let him. Carefully, she reached over to take her hands in his.

"Agent Richards. Are you alright? You don't seem yourself."

"I'm okay. Oh, it's not Agent, anymore, just Thomas Richards now. No more agent."

"Why? What happened? Don't tell me you quit?"

"My boss, he didn't appreciate me testifying against my partner. You'd think in the FBI the 'blue code of silence' would be nothing but a damn myth, but apparently, it was still alive and well in my unit and more important than protecting people or justice. He couldn't fire me, but he made it impossible for me to stay. I couldn't stand the hypocrisy. It's our job to protect our citizens by putting monsters away, and he was actually defending that son of a bitch."

"Oh, I'm so sorry to hear that." Her heart broke for him, knowing how badly it must have hurt to have his faith in the agency shattered like that. She squeezed his hands, wondering if he blamed her.

"Anyway, I just, I wanted to check on you, see if you were doing okay down here. You, you look like you're doing better."

"I am, I am. Thank you for thinking about me."

"No, please don't thank me." He touched her glasses briefly before continuing, "I'm sorry, I'm so, so sorry. I...I wish..."

Unable to take seeing him in such pain, Jessie moved closer and put her arms around his shoulders. "Shhh. It's alright. It's alright. It isn't your fault, not at all."

"But if I'd realized sooner…" Jessie realized he was crying now. "Oh, god, how could I have not seen it? I worked side by side with that man for ten years and didn't see him for what he was, and you suffered for it. I should have seen it. I should have known somehow. I should have stopped him. I should have protected you."

Jessie held him tight, rocking him slightly, making wordless sounds of comfort. For someone so dedicated to the job, she knew he must have been tearing himself apart ever since the day he'd discovered that his partner had become one of the very monsters he was supposed to hunt.

"I don't know how to make it up to you, to put things right. Testifying against him, losing my job, it just doesn't seem like it's enough. I even thought about eating my gun, but it felt like a cowardly thing to do when you were still out here dealing with far worse." His sobbing had gotten to the point she could barely understand him.

"It's okay, Thomas, it's okay." She continued rocking him, trying to find something to say to comfort him as her own hot tears ran down her cheeks. So many lives destroyed because of one man. When his crying quieted, she moved to squat down in front of him, forcing him to look at her.

"You listen to me, you listen. He betrayed you, the same as me, maybe more so because he was your partner. I can't even imagine how much more it hurt to have your boss do the same, because of some archaic and foolish idea that law enforcement is somehow above the law. But you didn't buy into that, and you lost a lot, but you still have your own self-respect. So, don't give in to the pain now. No matter what, because you remember, if nothing else, that if it weren't for you, I'd be dead now. You saved my life, and for that, I will always, always thank you."

She hugged him again, and this time he returned the embrace. Seeing he was calmer, she let go, taking his hands again, she put her forehead against his and whispered. "I realized over the last few weeks, before I could move on and find a future for myself, I had to forgive myself for anything I did to cause this, including trusting the wrong person. Whatever guilt you feel you may have here, I forgive you, I swear. So please, please try to forgive yourself."

They stayed quiet for a while, Jessie gently rubbing his back as he got himself back together. Finally, he chuckled a little. "I can't believe I just sat here and cried like that. There go all my cool points, eh?"

Laughing with him, Jessie shook her head. "Nope, I think men who can cry when they need instantly double them. It seems like you needed to let your feelings out some."

"Yeah, I guess so. Wasn't what I came here to do, at least, I don't think so. Truth be told, I don't remember much of the last week or so, or even coming out this way."

"It's Thanksgiving. Why don't you give your mom a call? I imagine she's pretty worried about you?"

"Yeah, you're right. I should give her a call."

She left to give him some privacy and joined her brothers in the kitchen, walking straight into James's arms, still hurting for him. Trying not to cry again, she told James a short version of what happened.

"Damn, I thought he looked like hell, but didn't think it was that bad." James kissed her forehead, always hating to see her cry. "Don't you cry, Lil' Bit. If it weren't for him…I don't even want to think about it. I'll call a few folks I know, see what we can do for him. You think he'll be okay?"

"I think so. He was bottling up everything inside, until it was just too much. I think, now that he's let it out, he'll be okay. I'm gonna give him some coffee and see if he's going to head to his mom's or maybe stay to have dinner with us."

They went back to the living room, where Richards was finishing up his call. His eyes seemed like he had cried again. "Mom started crying. Never could take hearing her cry. Said she's waiting for me, and to hurry up and get back home 'cause she's hungry."

Laughing, Jessie hugged him again. "Well then, you better get going. Will you be okay?"

"I think so, thanks to you."

As he headed back out to his car, James stopped him at the door and held out his hand to shake it. "I know things are tough for you, but you saved my sister's life. I promise it's a gift I will never forget you gave us. Thank you."

Richards stared a moment then grasped the hand he was offered. "I'd say we're even. I may have saved her life that day, but today, I think she may have saved mine."

"Maybe, but if I can ever return the favor, you just call." Shaking hands again, Richards headed back out to his car. Jessie came to the door to stand beside James as they watched him leave. "He'll be alright, sweetie. Just needed someone to help him remember who he was is all. Now, you might want to call Galen before he runs over here. Then we better get ready to go. It's almost time for dinner."

Chapter 26

GALEN PICKED UP BEFORE the first ring even finished. "Jess, everything okay? What's going on?"

She hated hearing the concern in his voice, but now wasn't the time to tell the whole story. "Yes, it's fine. It was an old friend from Chicago who stopped by to check on me. He'd changed cars since I saw him last, so that's why I didn't recognize it."

Galen's sigh was loud through the phone. "Why do I get the feeling there is a lot more to this story?"

"There is, but for now, can we leave it at that? I…I've done enough crying for this holiday and right now all I want is to get dressed so I can see you and Michael."

"Alright, for now. Do you want us to pick you up on the way?"

"Sure, that'd be nice. I'll go ahead and send James and Jack back to the restaurant. Give me, say, thirty minutes?"

"Okay, we'll see you then."

His voice still sounded annoyed as they hung up, but when she opened the door half an hour later, there was no trace of it as he gave an appreciative look at her long-sleeved black wrap. "Oh, boy."

"You like?" He stepped inside to pull her close, kissing her fiercely. Once, it might have frightened her, but now she welcomed and returned it.

"Do you know the kind of thoughts this dress puts in my head?"

"No…why don't you tell me?"

Kissing her again, he led her back outside. "We better go before I forget I have a little boy in the car and folks waiting for us." Giggling, Jessie followed. Jazza said the dress might inspire just such a reaction. With a mental note to thank her friend, Jessie decided the hot look in Galen's eyes made the dress well worth the slightly exorbitant price.

When they arrived, in addition to her siblings, Phillip, and the two Aria sisters, they saw Michael's friend Derek there with his mom, giving the boy someone his own age to talk to. Leaving Michael to chat with his friend, Galen followed Jessie into the kitchen to help carry the prepared dishes to the large tables in the middle of the main dining room where everything was set up buffet style.

As they started loading their plates and taking their seats, Galen recognized several other guests who had joined them while the food was set up. There were some other single parent families like Derek's mom, some older singles and couples, even some of the local loners had come out to join them. Some of the guests sat near the bigger family table set up for the Bradshaws and Arias, while others sat a bit apart, seemingly happy to be there, but also preferring to stay out of the main conversation.

Galen gave permission for Michael to sit with Derek so they could continue chatting, while he joined Jessie at the family table. This time, James and Jazza sat directly across from them. Despite his efforts, Galen couldn't catch the other man staring, but he could feel that cold, accessing gaze on him any time he wasn't looking at him.

When he'd joined the family before, it was simply as a friend, but now Galen knew it was obvious he was there as a true date. He'd put his hand on Jessie's back as they'd walked to the tables to fill their plates, quietly touched her fingers under the table, laid his arm across the back of her chair when he leaned in to catch something she said.

At one point, he did finally look up to see James practically glaring at him while Jessie was chatting with Silky, who was sitting to her other side. While he managed to hold the gaze, inside Galen felt an irrational urge to squirm and had to fight the instinct to look away. A full minute passed when James broke the spell with a slight jump before looking over a grinning Jazza who whispered something in his ear. Galen got the distinct impression she'd poked her lover for glaring at him. After James kissed the tip of her nose, he looked back at Galen with a more relaxed gaze.

"So, the renovations seem to be going well?"

"Yep," Galen replied with a smile. "Things are moving along nicely, though it helps that Jessie is pretty much the ideal client."

"Oh, how so?"

"Well, a lot of the delays that happen in renovations come more from issues with clients changing their minds, repeatedly, during the process. They have one idea, then see something else and decide they like it better, they don't fully think through a choice then realize it doesn't work once it's in place or in progress, or they just can't make up their mind even when it's time to make the final decision. I try to mitigate as much as I can during the planning process, but still, it happens more often than not, especially with residential work. But Jessie had done a lot of pre-planning, so she had great notes and had clearly thought through a lot of her choices already. We've only had to make minor adaptations due to more common issues, like discovering something when we open a wall or stocking issues."

At that James actually chuckled. "She always was a thorough researcher. It's what makes her so good at her job. In school she actually had issues with some of her papers being too long because she'd just had so many sources to include."

Realizing they were talking about her, Jessie turned back to them with a smile. "That was only twice, and I still got a great grade, just a note to be kind to the poor professor who had enough to read without extra. Anyway, it helps that Galen is also great to work with. He respected my choices rather than trying to push his own ideas onto me and is really good at explaining if an issue does come up with sensible options for dealing with it while still trying to stick to the spirit of what I had in mind. I think Grandpa would really love how the house is coming together."

"I'm sure he would." James returned her smile with one so filled with love and warmth it made Galen almost do a double-take. While he may be cold to the world, it was clear the man loved his family dearly, and that jumped Galen's like of him immensely. "I think that's why he left it to you, he knew you loved it and would be the one who could restore it while also breathing new life into it."

Galen was inclined to agree. He loved showing Jessie the progress on the house because it meant getting to see her look so adorably excited about how it was all coming together. Her obvious love of the house had long since erased any lingering feelings of regret Galen had over not being able to buy the house from her.

Later, as he was refilling his plate at the buffer, James joined him. "Thank you for letting Michael befriend Jessie. I think that and your helping with the renovation have both helped her come a long way since she came home. I just wanted you to know we appreciate it."

"I'm glad we could help, and that she ended up being part of our life. She's been pretty good for both of us, too." Galen paused, trying to decide how to approach the subject of their relationship, before settling on straight-honesty. "This feels odd for a man my age, and considering Jessie is a full-grown woman, but I know you raised her and so it almost feels like I should be asking if you're cool with us dating."

To his surprise, James laughed. "Sorry, Jazza said I was giving you the 'dad glare' earlier. I guess it's habit after all these years." He put his hand on Galen's shoulder. "From what I've seen, you've done her a world of good, helping her get back to normal. Long as you're good to her, then we're good too."

Galen nodded, relief flowing through him at having the air cleared, at least with regards to her brother. There was still the issue of whatever had happened in Chicago that had so broken her in the first place and the truth of her visitor earlier that day. While he was looking forward to their second date, he also knew at some point they would have to sit down and have a serious talk about her past if they were going to have any chance of having a future together.

Chapter 27

DURING THE HOURS leading up to her next date with Galen, Jessie was a bundle of nerves. Things were moving so fast, faster than she'd have ever expected. Part of her just wanted to enjoy things as they were, but Galen's kisses were becoming more insistent and it was clear that he wanted to eventually do more. It wasn't as if she didn't want the same. Her libido had certainly awakened with a vengeance since she'd started seeing Galen.

Still, in the background, she couldn't help being afraid of what might happen. She knew the statistics, the stories, what the hospital shrinks had said. So far, his kisses hadn't scared her, they'd been nothing but pleasurable, but he'd kissed her without touching her otherwise, except one brief embrace when he'd dropped her home after Thanksgiving dinner.

Should she tell him everything now, before it happened, or give heavier making out a try first in hopes that nothing bad happened? No, no, she had to tell him before things got to the point of trying to make love. There was no way to hide the scars along her body, and she couldn't bear the thought of him seeing them and being disgusted by what he saw. Hugging herself, Jessie walked around her room taking deep breaths, trying not to let her thoughts depress her.

She reminded herself of what Jazza had told her before. If it was meant to be, Galen would be able to accept it as part of who she was, and they'd find a way to make it work. If not, she knew that the healing she'd done through her friendship with Michael and her relationship with Galen, would remain with her even if he did decide he didn't want to continue associating with her in a romantic way.

She was also certain that Galen wouldn't be the kind of man who put an end to her friendship with Michael if their own relationship ended. She stopped in front of the mirror and looked at herself. No matter what, she would be okay now. Realizing it gave her a new-found sense of inner strength and confidence.

An hour before Galen was due to pick her up, he called to cancel. "I'm sorry, sweetie, but I'm afraid we're going to have to postpone our date. Michael has come down with a cold, so I need to stay here with him."

"Oh, will he be okay?"

"I think so. He has a slight fever though, so I want to keep an eye on him."

"Of course, of course. Is there anything I can do?"

"Not that I can think of but thank you for the offer."

After they disconnected, Jessie continued to worry. She knew it was probably silly, it was just a cold, right? But colds were miserable, with all that coughing, sneezing, and aching. Wanting to do something for her young friend, Jessie decided to follow the time-honored tradition of what to do when someone was sick: make some soup.

A quick check of the pantry and fridge left her disappointed. She didn't have enough ingredients to make a good chicken noodle soup, or really much of anything at all as the kitchen part of the remodel was due to start the following week so she'd avoided going to the store. It was tempting to just dismiss the idea of making soup, tell herself it couldn't be helped and that Galen would certainly feed his son fine without her help.

A warm, wet nose pressed itself against her hand. Jessie smiled down at Causy and gave her a pet. "Yeah. After all they have done for me these last few months, this isn't the time to give in to the old demons and backslide. Come on girl, let's go take the next step in our recovery."

Though she trembled at the thought of what was to come, Jessie bundled up then headed out to the car, Causy at her heels. A few minutes later, she was parked outside the grocery store, willing the shaking to stop. "I can do this, I know I can.

Time to prove that all the support we've been getting hasn't been misplaced!"

It was cold enough to safely leave Causy in the Pilot with the windows half down while she forced herself to walk into the store, grab a cart, and head for the produce section. When she'd come with Michael the first time, she'd been terrified and had to fight the urge to bolt more than once. Now she was happy to find the deep fear had lessened to a much more manageable level of anxiety. She managed to return the quick casual greetings of people passing by and to even look at the cashier instead of anywhere but.

Walking back to the car with her cart, she knew she was grinning from ear to ear, rightfully proud to have managed to accomplish her task on her own. Back home, she hummed to herself as she prepared the soup. For the first time in a long time, she was starting to feel more like herself.

Once the soup was done, she decided to drive to Galen's rather than walk and risk dropping the hot container. As she pulled into the drive, self-doubt started to eat into her earlier confidence. Would Galen be annoyed at her for stopping by unannounced? Maybe she should have called first?

The porch light came on, forcing her to push the doubts aside, grab the soup, then head to the door. He opened it before she could knock.

"Hey, is something wrong?"

"No, no, I'm sorry. I hope I'm not intruding, I just, well, I made some chicken noodle soup for Michael and thought I'd drop it by." Galen's warm smile wiped away her worries.

"Come on in. I bet he'll like your soup way more than the stuff I was about to heat up." He couldn't help laughing at Jessie's look of horror at the can sitting on the counter.

"Condensed? Canned? Oh, I'm glad I came by. Colds deserve good soup."

Galen tried to solemnly agree but couldn't stop chuckling. Giving up, he kissed her forehead before getting a bowl. "You, my dear, are a food snob."

"Am not, I just like real soup." She threw a grin at him over her shoulder.

After dishing up some soup, Galen put the bowl on a tray with crackers and juice and started up the stairs to Michael's room, inviting Jessie to come with him. Cautiously, she followed behind Galen, poking her head in as he went into Galen's room.

"Jessie, hey, you came to see me?" Michael looked a little tired and worn, but otherwise seemed all right as he sat up against his pillows to eat his soup. Feeling relieved, Jessie came closer.

"Yeah, I had to come save you from the evils of canned soup."

Laughing Michael looked at the bowl in front of him and quickly grabbed his spoon to try it. "Mmm. It's so good."

After Michael finished eating, Galen left them alone for a few minutes while he took the tray downstairs and prepared Michael's medicine.

"I hate that medicine, it's so nasty."

"Oh, I know, I don't like it much either. You know the secret to not tasting it?"

"No, is there one?"

"Yep, hold your nose while you gulp it down. If you can't smell it, you can't taste it."

"Huh?"

"Well, you know you have taste buds on your tongue, right?"

"Right…"

"Well, they don't work alone. They work with your nose to tell you what you taste. That's why food doesn't taste as good if your nose gets stopped up, because you can't smell it, so your brain doesn't know how to process the taste."

"Really? You're not just teasing me."

Laughing, Jessie raised her right hand and cross her left over her chest. "Girl Scout's honor."

"You were a Girl Scout?"

"Well…actually no." They were still laughing when Galen returned.

Trying Jessie's suggestion, Michael pinched his nose closed as he took the cup of green liquid from his dad and then quickly tipped it into his mouth and swallowed it in one gulp. He shuddered a little as he let go of his nose and handed the cup back to his father. "It was still pretty nasty, though I guess maybe it wasn't quite as bad as it usually is."

"Anything is worse than the usual taste, right?" Galen came over to tuck him in, letting him know it was time to go to sleep. He kissed his son goodnight and started to turn off the light, but Michael stopped him.

"Um, Dad, could Jessie maybe read me a story before I go to sleep." Michael looked at her to see if she would be willing to as well, while Jessie looked at Galen to see what his answer would be.

"Sure, son, if she wants to."

"Well then, I'd be honored. What book would you like to hear?" Michael handed her a well-worn book from his bed-side table. "Oh, Black Beauty? That's one of my favorites."

"Really?"

"Oh yes, I actually have several copies because I love it so much."

With a grin, Michael patted the space beside him. Galen headed to the door, standing just outside it for a little while to watch as Jessie sat beside Michael on the bed, opened the book to its bookmarked place and began reading.

Jessie was barely aware of him leaving to head downstairs and wait for her to finish. When she joined him later, she looked a little nervous. "He's sound asleep. I hope that was okay?"

"Of course, it was, it was…well, it was beautiful. Thank you. Why not sit down a bit? We didn't get to go out tonight, but since you're here, why waste the opportunity?" He'd sat on the sofa on purpose; enjoying a little fantasy about making out with her before remembering that things like that might scare her.

He was pleasantly surprised when she smiled mischievously, sitting close enough to press her leg against his. "Does your invitation only include sitting or did you have something else in mind?"

"Honey, I have a lot in mind, but what parts we do are up to you."

"I…I can't promise I'll be able to handle it, but…well, I'm willing to give it a try, if you are?"

Galen sat up a little and leaned closer. "Oh yes, I am. If you do get scared, just tell me and we'll stop, okay?" She was still nodding slowly as he touched her face with one hand, cupping her jaw and stroking her cheek with his thumb as his lips brushed across hers. With only a moment's hesitation, she brought her own hand up to touch his face, the tips of her fingers resting against his strong chin. He changed the angle of the kiss, deepening it, yet keeping it relaxed. His tongue teased her lips and she opened her mouth to allow him entry with a soft moan.

Slowly, giving her plenty of time to object should she want to, Galen moved his hand down to her neck, then stroked her arm before carefully moving back up to brush his knuckles across her breast. Encouraged by the little moan she made, he repeated the motion before fully stroking her openly with his hand, cupping her and using his fingers to gently tease her nipple under her shirt.

When Galen broke the kiss, she made a little-distressed sound, but his lips returned quickly, pressing against her jaw then her neck with a little sucking motion that made her arch against him with a pleased sigh.

"Oh, Galen." She felt him smile against her skin, as he moved down further, pressing kisses against the edge of her shirt. Lifting his head, he leaned back against the arm of the sofa, bringing one of his legs partly up on the sofa and gently pulling her with him so she leaned against him. Silently agreeing with the idea of getting more comfortable, Jessie shifted and pulled her legs up on the sofa, allowing him to stretch out more so she could lie against him as his lips reclaimed hers. With one hand, he trailed his fingers along her spine and stroked her back, while the other moved to tease her other breast. She could feel her nipples tighten in response to his sensual assault, pushing against the fabric and demanding he touch them more.

Reading her reactions like an artist, he adjusted the pressure and style of his touch, teaching himself how she liked to be touched and what strokes would elicit unguarded moans from her. His other hand moved down her back to cup her behind, bring her lower end more fully against him.

His own desire increasing with every touch, Galen wanted more. He wanted her lying beneath him as he pressed his mouth against the silky soft skin his hand was caressing. However, when he moved to pull up her shirt, Jessie's sound of distress had him quickly reversing the motion.

"It's okay, love, it's okay. Not that far yet. I understand." He kissed her gently while whispering comforting words. She soon calmed and returned his kisses with fervor, so he knew she hadn't shut down completely.

"I'm sorry."

"You don't need to be. I told you, this is your show, you set the pace." He brought one hand back up to gently stroke her cheek with his finger. "I know you'll tell me when you're ready." She smiled at his gentle words and pulled up to kiss him fiercely. In the back of her mind, she knew she had to talk to him soon, because she wanted to be able to take off that shirt, and more.

Chapter 28

THROUGHOUT THE WEEK, as work progressed on Jessie's house, she and Galen enjoyed flirting with one another whenever they could. Galen's men teased him relentlessly, loving the sight of their boss, who'd seemed formerly oblivious to women, act like a teenager with his first girlfriend. Jessie got her fair share as well from Jazza and even her brothers, but neither minded.

Michael was also a frequent visitor, with Jessie helping him with his homework and Kipper's training. She wondered if he was aware of the turn her relationship with his father had taken, but she wasn't sure if it was her place to bring it up. To her surprise, Michael casually brought it up himself later that week.

"So, things going okay with my dad?" he asked while working on a grammar sentence.

"What do you mean?" Jessie asked cautiously.

"Well, y'all are dating and stuff now, right?"

"Ah, yes, yes we are. I wasn't sure if he'd told you yet or not. Things are going well."

"Good, I don't think he's dated much before, so I wasn't sure if he actually knew how."

Laughing, Jessie tapped the end of his nose. "Yes, he does know how. Is it okay with you that we are dating? I mean…"

"Of course it is." Michael beamed at her, putting Jessie's worries to rest before he even finished speaking. "I like you and you're my friend. My dad smiles more now and so do you. So, seems like a good thing to me."

"Cool. Thanks, kiddo." Galen came by later to pick Michael up, not wanting him walking across the street in the early winter darkness. Before they left, Jessie pulled him aside to let him know she'd gotten Michael's blessing.

"I wondered if he had figured it out. I wasn't sure how to talk to him about it. Glad I don't need to break it to him but guess we should talk tonight, man to man, just to be sure. By the way, he's, um, gonna be spending the weekend at his best friend's house. A sleepover that I dare not call a sleepover because he thinks it's a 'girly' word." Galen shook his head at the idea. "Would you like to help a lonely dad out by sharing some takeout, maybe a movie…maybe a little necking on the couch?"

"You are incorrigible! Your place or mine?"

"Well, you do have the bigger television." Jessie couldn't argue with that. Not that Galen had a bad television; it was a high quality, thirty-six-inch set. However, one of the jobs that had been completed during the week had been the installation of Jessie's new fifty-inch wall-mounted LED flat-panel television.

"Works for me. Chinese?"

"Sounds good. See you in the morning."

Since Michael now knew, Galen didn't feel like he needed to go back in the house to give Jessie her kiss, though he did keep it tamer than what he would have given her had they been alone. Friday evening, he made up for it when she opened the door. When they came up for air, she moved back a little to let him in.

"Now that is my kind of hello. Hopefully accompanied by some spicy vegetable chicken and a ton of spring rolls?"

"But of course. I know better than to leave my woman hungry." He held up the bag as he entered.

"Good I'm starved. I subscribe to a couple of streaming services, let's see what's playing." Glancing back at the door, Jessie shivered. "Good thing I started the fireplace earlier, it is positively freezing out there. Perfect weather for staying in and snuggling."

"Keep that up and we might have to skip dinner."

After plating up their food and getting some drinks, they settled in the living room on the sofa. Flicking through the movie listings, they settled on historical adventure film they'd both heard good reviews about. By the time the film ended, their plates were empty, and they had moved from sitting near to one another, to lying spooned together on the sofa. Galen's arm draped across her waist, his fingers lightly stroking her stomach. Jessie stretched, deliberately leaning back so her body rubbed against his before sitting up. His sound of frustration made her smile as he sat up beside her.

"That was pretty good. More historically accurate than I would have thought."

"Not bad at all."

"So, how would you feel about a cup of hot chocolate?"

Galen appeared to think for a moment, then put his hands together under his chin. "Michael mentioned you'd made a fresh batch of brownies this week?" He looked so much like a pleading little boy that she nearly doubled over laughing before kissing him lightly and standing.

"Oh, come on you. I do believe he left you a few." In the kitchen, Jessie warmed the brownies for a few seconds in the microwave, melting the chocolate chunks sprinkled throughout them to a nice gooey consistency. With two steaming cups of hot chocolate and the brownies on a plate, they returned to the living room. One moment they were laughing, and the next, Jessie had stopped dead in her tracks. When they'd left the room, they'd left the television on. Returning they found the system had moved on to the next film, and on the screen, a woman was screaming as a man attacked her.

Seeing how pale Jessie had gone, Galen ran over to grab the remote and turn off the screen. In the unnatural silence that followed, Galen watched her as one might watch a skittish colt. She hadn't moved since stopping, but he could see her hand starting to shake. Afraid she would burn herself with the hot chocolate, he returned to where she stood and very carefully removed the cup from her hand, along with the brownie, and placed both on the coffee table beside his own.

He felt helpless, unsure what to do. He wanted to put his arm around her and bring her to the couch, but he wasn't sure how she'd react to his touch right now.

Finally, he moved closer and quietly asked, "Are you okay? Do you want to sit?" After a moment, she looked at him, and with tears welling in her eyes, she nodded and moved over to the sofa and sat down. Hesitating a moment, he sat near her, careful not to touch her yet.

"I'm sorry…it surprised me and…"

"It's okay, sweetheart, you just sit, take all the time you need." She looked at him, her eyes so sad it hurt him to look at.

"No, no, I don't think I can anymore. I've thought all week that we should talk, but I keep putting it off."

Galen went still, and his heart went cold at her words. Was she about to end their relationship? "Jess…"

"I like you, Galen, I really do. I think…I think I might even be falling in love with you. That's why, before we keep going like this, I feel like it's only fair to tell you about

Chicago, and why I grew so afraid, and why I still am at times."

With a sigh of relief, Galen carefully reached out his hand, glad when she took it in her own. "Honey, if you are ready to talk about, then I'm ready to listen. But no matter what you tell me, I promise, I'm not running away from this, from you. Because I know I'm falling in love with you, and I don't want to lose you. Whatever problems are left, we can deal with it, together."

Hearing that, she cried. His words were the ones she'd desperately hoped to hear. "Part of me was terrified you wouldn't want to know, much less stay." Even if he changed his mind, knowing he meant what he was saying now warmed her heart. Throwing her arms around him, she hugged him tightly for a moment then whispered, "Thank you." She pulled back and took a sip of her hot chocolate as if giving herself a shot of courage before beginning.

"I moved to Chicago after college, wanting a breather from my family. I love them, God knows I do, but back then, I felt like they suffocated me sometimes. They were always so protective. You know James didn't let me date in high school? It was only when I was in college and away from spying eyes that I finally went on my first date."

"Knowing your brother, that does not surprise me at all."

"Back then, I was just a single carefree girl living in a nice condo, well to do neighborhood, and naively thought I was safe from the world. Anyway, you remember how I told you that I do research, find information about people, places, stuff like that." When Galen nodded, she continued. "Sometimes my clients include law enforcement officials, with me maybe pulling together info on a possible suspect or on the victim of a crime, or even just some general info on a topic that might play into a case.

"Maybe a year and a half ago, Special Agent Curtis Crichton and his partner, Thomas Richards, came to me wanting information on a guy they suspected was a serial killer. There was a backlog with their own researchers and they needed to see where he'd been to tie his past travels to the dates and locations of the victims."

"Special Agents, as in FBI?"

"Yes. Took me maybe three days to get what they needed. With it, they knew without a doubt that he was the guy and they caught him. I never take on new clients without checking them out first and they both seemed okay. Crichton was your typical career agent, not spectacular, but did his job well and didn't have any bad marks. Richards was a hot shot, a little arrogant, but good at what he did. He was well on his way to being a top agent. Anyway, while working on the research, Crichton asked me on a date every one of those three days. I politely declined each time, of course.

"Four months later, they sought me out again for another case. Another couple of days of work, and of Crichton asking me out constantly and my turning him down. Even Richards had shook his head and asked him he was just a glutton for punishment. Crichton said he figured if he asked enough times, I'd eventually say yes. It was a little creepy, but still he seemed harmless, you know? I just wrote it off as a weird joke.

"Then, last October they had another job for me and we did the usual dance of Crichton asking me out and my declining. This time, trying to trace the past of a murder victim. She was new to town, so no one knew her. She didn't have a driver's license, and they couldn't even find out her social security number, just her name and address. She was living in a sketchy, low-rent place, but everyone there said she seemed nice, quiet, out of place. Took a while, but I finally found out who she was, and found her family so they could know what happened and could bury her. I passed on the information to the agents, and that seemed to be that."

Jessie wrapped her arms around herself, as if trying to shield herself from the memories. In the week after the case, she'd had a lot of hang up phone calls. Never anyone on the end and always untraceable. It had been a little unsettling, but she'd written it off as some new scam call making the rounds. When she started using her phone's screener option to deal with them, the calls had stopped.

A week after the case was done she'd taken herself out to dinner at one of her favorite Mexican restaurants. It was still relatively early when she left, but with the time of year, the sun had been down a while. Arriving home, she hadn't suspected anything was wrong. The door was locked tight, alarm set, hall light on because she hated coming home to a dark house.

Causy was at the vet's overnight for a dental cleaning, so the quiet condo seemed normal. Turning on the TV to her favorite music channel, she'd headed to her bedroom to change. She'd just laid her purse on the bed when he slipped out her closet and wrapped his arms around her.

"Welcome home, honey." She tried to scream when she heard Crichton's voice in her ear, but his hand came over her mouth. If there was one thing James Bradshaw had done, it was make all his siblings go through self-defense training, led by him. Jessie used every ounce of that training then, elbowing him in the stomach, trying to break free. He was surprised at the maneuver, and released his hold, but not for long.

Jessie kicked and punched with everything she had, but since moving she hadn't kept up with her training, and he was just as well trained, plus stronger and faster. Breaking free by throwing her alarm clock at him, she ran into the hall while cursing her love of privacy that had led her to choose a home with nearly soundproof walls. She could scream all she wanted, but unless someone was right outside the door, they wouldn't hear her.

She made it halfway down the hall before Crichton caught up with her, grabbing her by the ankle. As she fell to the floor, she caught herself on her hands and tried to kick back with her free leg. He struck her across the legs with something, sending pain screaming through her body. Pulling on her leg, he dragged her back towards him, causing her dress to bunch up around her waist. She felt him ripping her panties off even as she tried desperately to fight, to turn so she could swing at him, anything, but he held her down with his body.

When he shoved himself inside her, she couldn't stop the scream from escaping, nor the tears. He was brutal, thrusting into her as hard as he could, obviously enjoying the pain he caused. At first, she kept trying to fight, but she realized it was only exciting him more. He couldn't plan on letting her live; she knew exactly who he was.

Desperate, she went limp, pretending she'd fainted from the attack and waiting until he started to rise. Despite the pain, she managed to flip herself over and kick him in the groin. Sweeping his legs out from under him, she tried to scramble to her feet and run down the hall, but the leg he'd hit slowed her down.

"Naughty, naughty." He caught her easily, but before she could turn to fight, something stabbed her in the neck and everything went dark. When she woke up, she found herself tied to her bed, her arms tied together at the wrists to the headboard. Her feet were tied to the bedposts at the end of the bed, leaving her legs spread. Crichton was sitting in a chair beside the bed, naked and watching her.

"Rise and shine, love. I've been waiting for you."

"Why are you doing this? You're an FBI agent for god's sake, how can you do this?"

"Ah Jessie, my dear, I can do this because I'm an FBI agent. I can enjoy you as long as I want, and no one will question anything. When I'm done, no one will find you for a long, long

time." As he spoke, he sounded more and more insane. Jessie suddenly remembered a popular saying among those who dealt with violent criminals: "He who does battle with monsters needs to watch out lest he in the process become a monster himself. And if you stare too long into the abyss, the abyss will stare right back at you." Apparently, Crichton had crossed that line.

He approached the bed. Trussed up as she was, she couldn't even fight as he gagged her. When he was done, she wanted to vomit but knowing she'd only choke herself if she did, she made herself swallow it. Unable to escape, she tried to think of anything else but what he was doing.

Crichton held her there like that for a long time. The first day, he raped and sodomized her repeatedly. Knowing he intended to kill her, she kept trying to fight. The few times he left her alone, she strained at the ties, shredding the skin around her wrists. As the hours passed, he grew more violent, beating her while raping her and at times hitting her just to hit her.

Between his "visits," he made himself comfortable in her home, watching television and cooking meals. Her phone rang twice. The first time, he swiped it to ignore. The next time, later in the day, he laughed as he looked at the screen, before throwing it against the wall, shattering the screen and sending pieces of circuitry flying.

Jessie grew weaker, but in some ways, it was a blessing as she drifted in and out of consciousness making it easier to escape the pain. The living nightmare truly became hell on the second day. That was when Crichton brought out the knife, making little slashes along her entire body, her breasts, abdomen, legs, back, even across her buttocks and crotch.

During one of his sessions, he'd taunted her, "I bet you wish you'd accepted my date invitations now, eh, you stuck up bitch?" In defiance, Jessie spat at him. He retaliated by slashing the knife across her face, its blade cutting into her nose and running up diagonally, across her eye. It was then that her left eye lost the ability to see.

The bed was drenched in blood, its once white sheets forever stained a dark maroon. Jessie knew her life was slowly oozing away from her, and she found herself praying she would go soon while also crying that she wouldn't get to see her family one last time.

In her mind, she apologized to James for ignoring his advice on ways to secure her house, so she'd know if someone had been inside. Though she knew he'd never blame her, she cursed herself for it all the same. She wished she could see all her brothers and Jazza again, tell them she loved them and thank them for raising her. Most of all, she prayed there was a heaven so that at least she could see her mother again.

It was nearing dusk when she awakened to find him sitting on top of her, the knife in his hand and a particularly terrifying smile on his face.

"There you are, love. I didn't want you to miss this. My vacation days are over, so it's time for us to say goodbye, but don't worry, I like long goodbyes." He'd raised the knife up to stab her when a shout came from beside them.

"Drop the knife and get off her now." In the doorway to her room, Agent Richards stood, gun aimed at Crichton. Behind him, Jessie could see the shadows of several other men. For a moment, Crichton appeared as if he were going to stab her anyway, but he dropped the knife and laughed. He rose off her slowly and stood beside the bed. As they cuffed him, he looked at her, still laughing insanely. Richards cut the ties lose from her arms and legs and covered her with a blanket. Things had started going dark as she stared up at him. The last thing she heard was him whispering, "I'm sorry, oh God, I'm sorry."

Chapter 29

WHEN JESSIE LOOKED at Galen again, she ached to see tears streaking his cheeks. Gently, she reached up to wipe them away, afraid he wouldn't want her to touch him. But instead, he held her hand against his face. With his free hand, he reached out for her other hand and she gladly took it as she told the rest.

"They took me to the hospital and Crichton was arrested. I kind of faded in and out in the ambulance and while they worked on me, but I can remember seeing Richards there. He refused to leave me, even at the hospital. He stood nearby while doctors worked on me, and then watched through a window when they took me in to operate. I don't think he left until my family arrived.

"Other than that, I can remember laughing to myself when I heard the doctor yelling that he was out of stitching material and someone had to go get more. It was like I wasn't even there anymore but watching a weird television show and for some reason that made me laugh, though I know it wasn't funny. I can remember the sounds they made when they started examining my lower areas and doing the rape kit. It's hard to describe. It was more than horrified or pitying. I just remember it making me ache, so it didn't surprise me when they explained that I'd suffered so much internal damage that they had to do a hysterectomy."

She heard Galen sharply inhale, then felt him squeezed her hand. He seemed to know she needed to get it all out. "I was in the hospital for over a month. In addition to the knife wounds and internal injuries, he broke my leg when he hit me when I was trying to run. No wonder I couldn't get away again. Suffice to say, I never went back to my condo. After they released me, I retrieved Causy from the kennel where my brothers had placed her and moved into a hotel. It was good she wasn't home that night, he'd planned to kill her once I was captured, another way to torture me by watching her die." Jessie shuddered at the thought. "Anytime I left the hotel, I felt like everyone was staring at me, at the scars, so I started covering myself up. Then that incident in the restaurant, with the eye I couldn't so easily hide, and I stopped going out in public except to stand in the doorway while Causy did her business outside. Jazza and my brothers took turns staying with me, especially at first, but I finally made them go home. One still came once a week to check on me, bring anything I needed.

"I didn't want to be there anymore, but I didn't know where to go. Eventually, they told me about Grandpa dying. They hadn't told me at the hospital, not wanting to risk that I'd get so upset it would slow my recovery. I loved him, you know, just like he'd been my real grandfather. I felt awful that I hadn't been here for him. When they said that he'd left me his house, it was as if he was offering one last gift of love, a safe place to run too. As soon as I had finished testifying, I packed up and came here. James handled selling my condo, closing up my office, and getting rid of anything I left behind."

Galen didn't speak at first, just watched her before finally pulling her into his arms and holding her tight. He kissed her hair while making comforting sounds that had no words. After a few minutes, he pulled back and kissed her as tenderly as one might a baby, then swiped his thumb across the tears on her face, tears she hadn't realized had been falling since she'd started.

"That you could let me into your life, let me touch you, let me kiss you after that. I feel so honored and so humbled. I…I can't even imagine going through that, much less surviving it."

This time she kissed him, a kiss filled with gratitude. "It could have only been you, only you." For a while, they held one another, occasionally sharing soft exploratory kisses, each as sweetly hesitant as if it was the first time.

Eventually, Galen recalled one of the last parts of the story and frowned in confusion. "One thing I don't understand. Why did you have to testify? They caught him in the act, what could there be to say after that?"

Jessie pulled back a little, though stayed close as she tried to figure out how to explain it. "Crichton refused to plead guilty. At first, we thought he was planning to try the whole not-guilty-by-reason-of-insanity defense, but he didn't. He claimed I'd asked him to do it, that I'd been enjoying it, and that it was just a misunderstanding."

"What? Right, you asked him to hurt you like that? You asked him to kill you? No one would buy that."

"That's what the prosecutor said. Crichton's first lawyer even quit, refusing to play out his defense. The second one did as well. His third lawyer changed tactics, saying it had started consensual and just got out of hand, in hopes of getting the kidnapping charge dropped and the attempted first-degree murder charge reduced. I think Crichton himself knows it's pointless, but it was one final way to hurt me and to hurt Richards. After he was arrested, the police discovered he intended to frame Richards for my murder and was going to kill him and make it look like a suicide. When he laughed about the phone call, it was Richards calling me because he'd gotten concerned. Crichton saw it as a perfect planting of evidence."

Galen cursed Crichton under his breath. Jessie nodded, understanding how hard it was to come up with any other word to describe someone so evil. "His lawyer is good, one of those high-priced asses trying to make a name for himself by freeing the big FBI agent from a clearly guilty charge. He managed to throw out some evidence on technicalities. Even went and found an ex-boyfriend of mine and had him on the stand, claiming I was a masochist, but the guy quickly recanted and apologized, said the lawyer threatened him."

"Ugh, I hate those kinds of lawyers. They give the rest bad names and then some. So, it sounds like the trial isn't over?"

"Yes, there is a lot of testimony and evidence to work through, as the prosecution is determined to prove he planned this for months, so the first-degree charges stick. It should be over soon, though. James told me they are in closing arguments now. I know they have been airing it on one of those trial coverage networks, but I can't bring myself to watch it."

"I don't blame you, not at all." He paused then gave her a small smile. "We must look a mess, both of us crying, but the thought of you going through that, in so much pain, it just hurt so much it was either cry or break something."

Jessie kissed him again and then rested her head on his shoulder. "Thank you, for hurting for me, for not looking at me like a monster or some broken pitiful thing. Thank you for being here."

"Always, love, always." He pulled her close again and Jessie was happy to rest in his arms. After a moment, he cleared his throat and spoke again. "Sweetheart, I…I still want to see you. I still want to make love to you, maybe even more so. I just want you to know that."

As she listened to his heart beating, she knew in that moment, she no longer had to wonder if she was falling in love. Feeling as if the last bits of ice melted from her heart, Jessie decided it was time to take back her life and stop allowing Crichton to ruin it. She stood and reached out her hand to him. "I can't promise I won't have a reaction, but if you're willing to try, so am I."

"Jessie." He took her hand and stood. With his answer clear in his eyes, she led him upstairs to the guest room, only slightly regretting she couldn't yet lead him to her own room which was still in progress. Leaving Causy in the hall, she closed the door behind them and gestured for Galen to sit on the bed. His eyes never left her as she stood in front of him and took a steadying breath. Quickly, she pulled her shirt up over her head, then threw it to the floor to avoid the temptation of trying to hide behind it.

Galen reached out to her, his fingers lightly touching the white scars that striped her stomach. Coaxing her forward, he followed his fingers with his lips, causing her to catch her breath. As if trying to make the wounds better, he lightly touched and kissed each one, first on her stomach, then her arms.

He reached up and slowly removed her bra, so his lips could kiss the streaks across her breasts. With one arm around her waist, he took one dusty colored nipple in his mouth, gently suckling it and lathing it with his tongue. When he'd brought it to a tight bud, he turned to the other to give it the same treatment. Jessie kept one hand on his head, playing her fingers through his hair as her body responded to his lovemaking.

His lips returned to hers, telling her without words that he still found her attractive and that he wanted her. Looking up at her from the bed, his eyes were darkened with desire. Not wanting to hold back anymore, Jessie moved away long enough to remove the rest of her clothes, then returned to his waiting arms. He kissed her stomach again, his tongue playing with her belly button while his fingers lightly moved across her butt and along her legs.

When he moved further down, kissing the junction at her thighs, she cried out his name. Digging both hands into his hair, she could only throw back her head and enjoy the pleasure pouring through her as his tongue delved between her folds, dipping inside her then back out to flick across her tight bud. He alternated, his finger in one spot, his tongue in another, and the dueling sensations sent her body into overdrive. He kept his free arm tightly around her as if sensing her legs were going weak. Her orgasm came quickly, without mercy, leaving her moaning as her body tightened, then went limp in release.

"Galen." She straddled him on the bed, kissing him deeply, the taste of herself on his lips only fueling her unspent desire. His hands moved over her restlessly, from her back to her breasts to her stomach, to her butt, to tease her quivering flesh. When she started pulling at his shirt, he quickly threw it off then fell back on the bed, allowing her full access to his body and she gladly accepted it. She ran her hands over his chest, then her lips, loving the way he quivered at her touch, and the way he moaned when she licked and sucked his nipples.

With a groan, he pulled her up to capture her mouth again, his kiss hot and hungry. When they finally came up for air, he looked at her questioningly. When she nodded, he quickly stood and stripped off his pants and underwear before returning to the bed. He lay down again then pulled her to him for another heated open-mouthed kiss. Jessie ran her hands down his torso, lips trailing little kisses across his collar bone, over each rib. When she reached his waist, she turned to stare at his member standing so proudly up from his body.

With slight hesitation, she reached out and ran her finger along its length, smiling as it twitched in response. His skin felt velvety soft, and she delighted in exploring the hard shaft and sensitive head. Out of the corner of her eye, she could see Galen desperately gripping the sheets. Feeling infinitely female as she realized she was tormenting him, she moved back up to kiss him. "I'm ready."

He didn't have to ask what she meant. Jessie shifted so that she was straddling him as he rose up slightly on his hands. For a moment, she stilled as he reached between them to position himself for her. Looking into his eyes, the brief flash-back passed, and she took him inside. She shifted back up, then down again, taking in a little more. Over and over, she worked her way down his shaft while he murmured words of encouragement.

With a gasp, she took him fully inside herself, then paused to fully enjoy the sensation. Galen's arms came around her, and he kissed her neck, her cheek, her lips. His hands touched her glasses but stopped there, waiting for her to answer. With a shudder, she knew it was time. After she whispered her consent, he removed the glasses and carefully placed them on the pillow beside them. She closed her eyes, waiting for some verbal reaction, then she felt his lips as they touched her scared skin, silently telling her that it hadn't changed anything.

"Ride me, love, ride me." His hoarse whisper making his desire clear. She complied and began to shift her body up and down. The way he had positioned himself meant that with each stroke, she got the double pleasure of feeling him sliding along her inner spaces and of feeling his body rubbing against the sensitive nub above. His rapid breath matched her own as she increased the pace. His fingers tightened on her hips, and she buried her hands in his hair as the familiar tension built. When it broke, she cried out his name, her body convulsing around him. Galen thrust twice more before joining her, calling out as his own orgasm rushed through him. As they fell back together on the bed, he kissed her softly and whispered her name.

Chapter 30

IT WAS STILL DARK outside when Jessie slipped out of the warm cocoon of Galen's embrace to go to the bathroom. When she was done, she headed downstairs to start the coffee, Causy padding along patiently behind her after getting a good morning petting. She knew from their previous conversations, and common sense considering his trade, that he was likely an early riser and would be grateful for the caffeine.

Fresh cup in hand, she made her way out to the porch, sitting on the rope swing as Causy settled at her feet. With a gentle nudge, the swing swayed in the low light of the rising sun as she contemplated the night before. She had her share of lovers, she was a healthy woman and over thirty after all.

And yet, never could she remember a man making her feel as cherished as she had when Galen had made love to her. The first time, his tenderness and letting her take the lead had helped her bulldoze past the flashbacks. And then the second, when he'd reached for her in the middle of the night, despite his clear need for her, he'd gone painstakingly slow and patient to avoid causing her fear. When he'd finally slid inside her, she'd been so full of longing all she could think of was him, the beautiful man on top of her, inside her, whispering his longing even as his hands had backed up his words.

She'd thought before that she was falling in love with him, but any lingering doubts about her feelings fled during their lovemaking. To her surprise, the thought of falling in love didn't make her feel anxious or uneasy, nor did she feel any of the adolescent clinginess she remembered from her "serious" boyfriends of long ago. If anything, it gave her a feeling of peace, of truly being home at last.

While she didn't yet know how Galen felt, or what kind of future he saw with her, she couldn't seem to make herself dwell on it, at least not right then. For now, she would just enjoy it, this wonderful feeling of being in love, of having a new lover. It felt almost as if she was finally free.

She'd never forget what Crichton had done to her, of course, and she knew she still had some work to do to heal. There would always be the risk of flashbacks, of anxiety, and of course the physical scars would be there the rest of her life. But as dawn brightened the horizon, the weight of the attack seemed to bodily lift from her shoulders and float away on the gentle breeze that teased her hair.

Causy lifted her head to stare at the door, announcing Galen's awakening a few moments before he pushed open the screen, his own cup of coffee in hand.

"Mind if I join you?" he asked, his voice sounding almost shy.

She smiled at him and patted the swing bench beside her. "I'd be disappointed if you left me to enjoy this beautiful sunrise all alone."

As he settled beside her, he turned to steal a kiss, which she freely gave. "Good morning, love. How are you feeling?"

Jessie chuckled. "A little tender, to be honest, but in all the best ways, I promise."

His grin was so full of pride as he wiggled his eyebrows at her that she laughed out loud. "Apparently, my body seems to think we're teenagers again, so, um, I don't suppose I could sweet talk you into coming back to bed for a bit."

With a laugh, Jessie stood and grabbed his hand, half pulling him into the house. "It would be a shame to let all that energy to go waste."

Two long hours later, she half skipped back into the kitchen. She swore Causy was looking at her in bemusement as she settled into her spot to wait for breakfast. "Oh hush you, you'd have said yes too." Jessie teased with a grin, before turning to the more serious task of whipping up waffle batter and pulling out bacon and eggs to make Galen a good breakfast.

Spending the day making love was a lovely, romantic idea, but their growling stomachs had reminded them that dinner the night before had been a long way off. Plus, she knew he had to leave before long to go pick Michael up from his friend's house and it was almost time for her session with Thor

She was just setting down their plates when Galen strolled into the kitchen from his shower and kissed her soundly before taking a seat. "Oh my god, you are a goddess. Is that a magic stove? Maybe we should keep it if this is the stuff it can produce?"

With a laugh, she joined him at the table. "You think this is great, just wait till you see what I can do with my shiny new kitchen. It is supposed to get going this week, or so I've heard."

Galen made several appreciative hums as he sampled everything on his plate before answering. "Yep, Monday morning you're going to have to switch to take out for a bit. It will probably take most of two weeks to finish up to the point you can cook in here again. I mean, the old fridge will be the living room temporarily, like we discussed, and you'll have a working microwave, but still. Are you sure you want to stick around for this part of things?"

"Yeah. I mean, I'm doing better, but still, where would I go? I'm not sure I'm quite up to staying at the local extended stay hotel. Moving back to the family house would just make James worry, and while Jazza would welcome me with open arms, her place is just a one-bedroom apartment."

He paused with his fork halfway to his mouth. "You, um, you could maybe come and stay over at our place. I mean, if you wanted to."

She smiled and covered his hand with her own. "That is incredibly sweet of you to offer, and part of me would love to say yes, but I think it's probably better for Michael that we hold off on doing anything like that for now. Not until we're sure where this is all going, you know?"

Though he looked less than happy about it, Galen nodded in agreement. "Yeah, I guess that is true. I mean, he knows we're seeing each other, but I haven't really talked with him about it yet." He put his fork down. "But just so you and I are clear, I have a pretty good idea of where I'd like this to go. Now, I know you may need some time deciding too, but, well, when you're ready, I hope you'll be thinking along the same lines."

They finished their breakfast in relative quiet, each lost in their own thoughts. When they were done, she walked him to the door so he could head home to change before picking up Michael. As they kissed goodbye, she put a hand on his shoulder to stop him. "Galen, I…I want to enjoy this, the fun together, the flirting, the teasing together. I can't even describe what I feel when I'm with you. So, I just want you to be clear, we probably are thinking along the same lines, just maybe a little different in speed, that's all.

Galen kissed her again, his lips brushing hers with aching tenderness. "I can live with that." He walked to his truck and opened the door, then stopped to look over it with a rakish grin. "Meanwhile, I guess I'll get to have some fun figuring out how to sneak over here for some good old-fashioned necking time."

She was still laughing as he drove down the drive and turned onto the road.

Chapter 31

JESSIE SPENT MOST OF the afternoon preparing for the work that would start on the kitchen on Monday. She cooked up several casseroles and soups using the foods that would likely spoil during the two to three-week time frame. While the dishes were in the oven, she carefully stowed her cookware, dishes, and flatware in the boxes Galen had helpfully brought her Friday. She stacked them neatly in her home office, where they'd be out of the way of the workers and potential accidents.

At five, she headed outside to work with Thor, leaving Causy in a stay on the porch. She'd stuck to a strict schedule with him, hoping the routine would help calm in down. He was standing at the kennel door, waiting for her. Though he didn't growl or bark, his muscles remained as tense as they'd been that first day. She also still couldn't bring Causy too close without him raging. Disheartened at the lack of significant progress, she still greeted him cheerfully as she reached for the leash and muzzle she kept him on during their training.

"Hey boy. How are you feeling today, huh? Ready to go through your paces?" She kept up a low-key conversation with him as she eased inside the kennel, slipped the muzzle on, and then led him outside. The training lead gave them enough room to work with, without risking him deciding to bolt.

She led him through several rounds of his obedience commands, including sit, stay, and recall. Most he did automatically, but when she commanded him to lie down he hesitated, whining under his breath as he shied away from the indicated spot.

"Thor, *platz.*" She repeated the command in a firm, but calm voice.

She could see him shaking as he whined again, before reluctantly easing down into the indicated position. She praised him and released him immediately, not wanting to force him into to stay in a position that clearly caused him anxiety. That was something to work on. She called him into a heel, then led him around the yard until he finally started to relax.

"That's a boy. You're okay, you're with friends. It will be okay. I'm not giving up on you, not yet. We'll just keep taking it one day at a time." Finally, she returned him to his kennel, then gave him his dinner before leaving him for the night to go do more research, see if there was something more she could be doing for him.

In the morning, Jessie was waiting on the porch to greet Galen and the crew as they arrived. Her anxiety was finally at a manageable level to let her stop being rude to the good men who were fixing up her house. With a grin, Galen ran up to the porch and kissed her good morning, in full view of his crew, who hooted and whistled at them.

"Sorry." He sounded anything but apologetic.

Returning his grin, she winked him. "Might as well give them a proper show then." She returned his kiss in spades, before swatting him away to get to work.

"You heard the lady, boys, let's get to it!" Galen yelled as he waved the crews on while grinning ear to ear. Two groups followed him into the house past Jessie, a few of the men still laughing as they said good morning on their way in. One was the group she'd already met who were working on her bedroom, the second would be the ones working on her kitchen, and she made sure to thank them again before heading into her home office to work.

Galen followed her in, unable to resist stealing some time with her before getting to work. "Busy day today?" He asked conversationally.

"Two background checks to run, and doing more research on training techniques, see if I can't reach out to some trainers for any more ideas."

"Still no major change, huh?"

Jessie felt herself tear up, and seconds later she was wrapped in his arms. "I just don't know what else to do. I've known him since he was a little ball of fluff with floppy ears too big for his head. I was there when he proudly completed his canine good citizen exam and when he was sworn in as an officer. I know it's probably hopeless, he isn't improving any at all, but still, I just…"

"You don't want to give up on him," Galen finished for her. "I understand. He's practically family and you aren't the kind of person who gives up easily. Even if it comes to the worse, you gotta know you did all you could, sweetheart, he couldn't have a better champion in his quarter."

She knew he was right, but she also knew Galen still had to keep his men away from that side of the house. Thor had raged the entire time they had worked on the last of the siding the other week, and the other day man had forgotten and gotten too close while looking for a spot to eat sending the dog into an incredible fury.

That evening as she took Thor through his paces once the men were gone, she tried to force herself to look at him with fresh eyes. He continued to whine and shy away when she ordered him into a down, and the second time, he seemed on the edge of refusing all together. From what she'd read, she suspected it was because he'd been ordered into a down just before the shooting had started, leaving him associating the command with what happened to him.

While he still hadn't shown any violence towards her and even asked for petting sometimes, she knew she couldn't just write off the incident with the worker as being an isolated incident or his reacting out of some feeling of guardship. He was in full, uncontrolled attack mode and the only thing that had saved that man from serious scars, possibly even death, was Thor being in that kennel.

It was Michael's visit that Thursday, right at six as usual so he wouldn't interrupt her at work or when she was working with Thor, that tilted the scales she hadn't fully realized she'd been measuring. Making a mental note to call the veterinarian in the morning to make the appointment, she pushed the bolt of pain that speared through her out of her mind. For now, she smiled at Michael and welcome him inside, deciding it would be better to talk with Galen first to decide how they would explain it all to Michael together.

Helping him with history homework took her mind off what she had to do, and it made her happy to see how much he enjoyed the topic now. He'd told her before it was his least favorite subject, but together she'd help him see the stories behind the history that made it much more fun to learn about.

With her own thoughts so distracted, it wasn't until after they were done and she was making them dinner that she realized Michael was sitting, staring at his feet, rather than keeping up his usual cheerful chatter.

"Is anything wrong?" she finally asked. When he nodded and looked up at her as if he wanted to cry, she moved her chair closer to his and sat in front of him.

"What is it, sweetie, what's going on?"

"I'm not sure. I think my friends Derek and Tyler are mad at me. They've barely talked to me all week, and then today, they were flat out ignoring me. When I talked to them, they made a big show of turning away and talking to each other. I don't even know what I did wrong. I mean, things were fine when we slept over this past weekend, we had a lot of fun as usual. And then suddenly they are all mad at me?"

"That does seem rather strange. Neither of them said anything that might give you an idea about what's bothering them?" He shook his head no. "Well, I think the best thing to do would be to get them to talk to you. Maybe just tell them, 'Look, guys, if I did something to make you mad, just tell me so we can work things out.' If they are your friends, I'm sure they want to make up too, so if you offer them an opening to air their grievances, they will probably respond. Of course, you have to be ready to hear them."

"Okay…what are grievances?" Laughing, Jessie explained that they were complaints people had. "Ah, so if I ask them to tell me what's bugging them, they are more likely to tell me than if I just wait for them to do it themselves?"

"Yep, you got it."

"Cool, I'll try that, thanks."

"No problem."

Chapter 32

WHEN MICHAEL CAME over the next day, Jessie was waiting with the ubiquitous hot chocolate to hear how his talk with his friends had gone.

He shuffled his feet under the table a moment before answering. "So, um…apparently they are mad at me about you."

Of all the things she'd been thinking could cause a tiff between pre-teen boys, it being her had never entered her mind. "Wait, over me? Why?"

"Well, I asked them like you said, and at first they acted like they were going to ignore me again, and then Derek got mad and said it wasn't like I had time for them anyway, because I was too busy with you."

"Oh, I see." It occurred to her that before she'd met Michael, he'd probably spent several afternoons with his friends, either talking on the phone or hanging out at their house. Other than the sleep over, she couldn't remember him spending as much time with them outside of school since she'd entered the picture though.

"Anyway, I tried to tell them that we're friends, same as I am friends with them, but then Derek said some stuff about you that got me mad. It really made me so mad, I wanted to hit him. But my dad has told me so many times that good men don't just jump to using their fists when their angry, so I made myself calm down."

"Good, I'm glad to hear it. I mean, yes, there are times when you may find yourself with no choice but to fight, but most of the time, it's better to try to talk the situation out if you can. So what did you do instead?"

"I told them they were wrong about you and that they should just come meet you themselves, then they would see you were cool and we could all be friends."

"Well, that's fine. I'd love to meet your friends." Michael looked down at the floor and the foot shuffling resumed. "Michael?"

"Um…so the thing is, I kinda said they could come over tomorrow to meet you." He looked up at her before continuing rapidly. "I'm sorry, I know I should have asked you first, but I thought they would just say forget it if we didn't do it soon. I'm sorry."

Jessie hesitated a moment. Thor was scheduled to be put to sleep early Monday morning. She'd intended to spend time with him, letting him enjoy the bits of family life he still could. She needed to write the obituary the police department had requested so they could release it along with information about his funeral when they announced his passing. At least they were considering his pending death to be in the line of duty, a result of the injuries he'd suffered from trying to save his handler.

Still, looking at Michael's pleading face, she didn't have the heart to tell him no. "Well, you're right, you should have asked first, but still, it's okay. I have time."

"Really? Oh, thank you!"

However, on Saturday Derek and Tyler didn't show up at the Andrews house at the time they were supposed to. Fifteen minutes after they were due, and having watched Michael looking out the windows every few minutes, Galen asked where his friends were.

"I'm not sure, Dad, I called their houses and they left already, so I guess they are running late."

"Hmm…well, if they don't show up soon, we can take a ride down the road and pick them up."

"Okay. Thanks, Dad." Michael went outside with Kipper to wait for them. Looking down at Jessie's house, he thought he saw something moving in her yard. Huh? *Derek wears a bright purple jacket like that.* Thinking maybe his friends had misunderstood the plan and had gone straight to Jessie's, he yelled into the house to let his dad know he was going over there. Part way up the drive, he spotted them coming from around the far side of Jessie's house.

"Hey, guys. I thought y'all were coming to my house first?"

"Oh, um, is that what we planned? We thought we were supposed to come here first."

"It's okay. What were you doing over there though?"

"Looking for you since you weren't out here." Derek sounded a little nervous.

Michael shrugged. It wasn't worth arguing over. "Well, come on then, we might as well go ahead inside since we're here."

Michael was fifteen feet from the porch when a movement to his left caught his attention and caused him to freeze. Standing at the corner of the house was Thor, his head down and teeth bared. The dog growled low in his throat and began moving slowly towards Michael. Remembering his talks with Jessie about dog behavior, he knew Thor was serious.

"Hey, Michael, what's wrong?" Derek asked.

"What did you do, Derek?" Michael answered, taking care not to turn away from the dog or raise his voice.

He heard a gasp from the porch. "Holy cow…run man, get up here now." Derek called out.

Michael ignored them. *Never run from a threatening dog, it will only increase their drive to attack.* Instead he replied in the same quiet voice. "Go inside, get Jessie."

He heard the door open, knowing they'd complied. Trying to avoid any sudden moves, he tried to talk calmly to Thor, telling him everything was okay and that he didn't mean any harm. He tried calling out a command, remembering Jessie telling him it could trigger their training instinct if a dog's bloodlust wasn't up, but Thor didn't obey.

As if realizing something was wrong, Kipper positioned himself between Michael and the growling dog, barking sharply. Michael wanted to pull him behind, knowing the young pup was no match for the more powerful dog, but not daring to risk startling Thor. Behind, he heard a car pull into the drive.

Galen had followed Michael over after wondering why Jessie hadn't called if Derek and Tyler were there. Seeing the dog threatening his son, Galen wanted to rush out of the car and grab Michael up in his arms, but his instincts told him that would only set the dog off. Jessie came out of the house with Causy and two obviously terrified little boys behind her. In her hands, she carried a rifle. Jessie came down the steps but didn't try to walk any closer to Michael.

"It's okay, honey, you're doing good. Stay right there and don't make any sudden moves, okay? I'm gonna try to get him back in his kennel."

"Okay." Michael said, his voice shaking.

Jessie called out to Thor, giving him the "at ease" command. The dog didn't obey but momentarily halted his advance, now only thirty feet from Michael. Jessie called to him to sit, which he obeyed, but only for a moment. With a whining snarl, he rose back to his feet.

Before anyone could stop him, Derek jumped off the porch, grabbed a rock, and threw it at the shepherd. "Go away you stupid dog!"

It was all the trigger Thor needed. With a snarl, he ran forward at top speed, heading straight at Michael. Galen ran towards his son as he spotted Jessie raising the rifle to her shoulder. But Jessie suddenly lowered it again, as Thor crashed not into Michael, but a massive ball of fur and muscle. Causy, who'd been standing beside Jessie and watching the scene unfold, had flown into action when Thor moved towards Michael. She threw herself at the attacking dog. When her weight hit Thor, it threw him backward, but he quickly regained his feet, and turned his rage on her.

Galen hugged his son tight and Jessie ran to join them while watching the fight. Causy had pure weight and power on her side, but Thor was faster and fueled by rage, keeping the match even. Jessie sent Galen and Michael up on the porch, then raised the rifle again and took careful aim. She called out to Causy to move away. Instantly, Causy made a huge leap sideways landing two feet away from Thor. Whispering that she was sorry, Jessie fired. With a yelp, Thor spun around, landing dead on the ground.

Causy trotted back to her mistress, and Jessie quickly checked to make sure her wounds were only superficial. Crying, she walked over to Thor's body and squatted down, gently stroking his fur. His own face soaked with tears, Michael ran over to Jessie and threw his arms around her.

"Oh honey, you okay?" she asked.

"Yeah. I'm sorry, I'm really sorry."

"Me too, sweetie, me too." She kissed his forehead, grateful beyond words that Michael hadn't been hurt. "At least now he can be at peace."

Galen joined and put his arms around them both holding them so tight it was a wonder they didn't break. Hand in hand, the trio walked back to the porch where Derek and Tyler waited. Through their sobs, they both apologized to Jessie and to Michael for pulling such a tragic prank.

Jessie rubbed their heads and told them it was okay. It was obvious the boys had learned their lesson, and she couldn't help feeling guilty for it happening as well. She invited them all inside while she called Julian to let him know what had happened.

While they waited for Thor's body to be retrieved, Galen helped Jessie serve up glasses of milk and a plate of cookies for the kids. Taking her aside while the boys ate, he hugged her and thanked her for saving his son. "Oh Galen, I'd die before I'd let anything happen to that little boy."

"I know, love, I know." He kissed away her tears, holding her tight.

Chapter 33

THOR WAS BURIED AT the Cascade Falls police cemetery beside his partner a few days later. Galen helped Jessie set up a planter in the spot where Thor had died. She and Michael planted white tulips inside it, representing Thor's devotion to his partner and the forgiveness he was given after his death.

After initially refusing to talk to them, Michael forgave his friends, who repeatedly apologized to both him and Jessie. Despite the way they met, his friends agreed that Jessie was pretty cool, as she hadn't yelled at them and instead had given them cookies and comfort. Over the week, Michael came by every evening to check on Jessie and it helped him feel better about the dog's death. He knew Thor wasn't really a bad dog.

Like Jessie, he'd hoped he could be helped and mourned his death.

Later the same week, the trial ended. Crichton was found guilty of aggravated battery, aggravated sexual assault, and attempted murder, but his lawyer had done his job well and managed to convince the jury that Crichton had snapped, getting them to go for the lower class felonies on the charges. The jury also acquitted him on the charges of official misconduct and came back hung on the kidnapping charge.

The following week, Galen left Michael with Phillip while he went to Jessie's house to sit with her as Crichton was sentenced. Normally, it would have taken over a month for the sentencing hearing to be held, but perhaps because of the high-profile nature of the trial, Crichton's was pushed ahead in the schedule. Jessie sat on the sofa, with Galen holding her hand and Jazza on her other side. Jack, Julian, and Julianna were also there, sitting around the room, while they watched the court channel covering the trial live. Only James was missing, having been called out of town unexpectedly.

Jessie held her breath as the judge began announcing the sentence. "Fifteen years?" Her jaw dropped in disbelief. "Did I hear right, that's all? That's all?"

Galen cursed under his breath and then pulled her to him when her crying became incoherent. After all that bastard did to her, a life sentence wouldn't have been enough, but such a short sentence? He could be out in less than half that if he made parole.

Jazza and Julianna also tried to comfort her, while Julian gave voice to his own anger and frustration. Galen noticed that Jack was relatively calm, which surprised him because he'd kind of thought Jack would be more hot-headed. Instead, Jack stood and quietly did something with his phone. Probably sending a message to James to let him know since he wouldn't be able to see the coverage in whatever country he'd traveled to for his work. From what he knew of James, he doubted Jessie's oldest brother would be very happy to see that message.

On the screen, Crichton was being led out of the courtroom, smiling as if he had won. In a way, Galen guessed he had, because he hadn't received the maximum time he should have, nor the life sentence he deserved. Suddenly, a loud sound came from the screen and then chaos bloomed at the courthouse, with several screams coming through the now shaky movements of the camera.

Jessie looked up in confusion. "What happened?"

"I'm not sure." Galen stared at the screen, trying to decipher the chaotic scene. "Hey, where's Crichton? Did they take him back inside?"

The on-screen confusion continued for a few more minutes, with the anchor of the show calling the reporter's name several times before she finally reappeared. "Sorry about that. We're okay." Visibly relieved, the anchor asked what happened. "We were here at the Chicago Criminal Courthouse where former FBI agent Curtis Crichton was being sentenced for his attack on a woman last year. As Crichton was led outside after being sentenced to fifteen years, two shots rang out. It appears they struck Crichton and we've be told that the shots were fatal. Police and FBI are still searching for the unknown shooter."

For a moment, no one in the room moved. Jessie slowly exhaled. "He's…he's dead?"

"Yes, sweetheart, he's…someone killed him. He's dead. It's over." Galen briefly wondered who might have been behind Crichton's death. While he wasn't an expert, he was pretty sure that two shots expertly fired into a group that size that only hit the target had to be the work of an accomplished sniper. Had Crichton's former partner, Richards, decided to make sure he paid for his crime?

In either case, Galen couldn't pretend he wasn't glad. With Crichton dead, Jessie would truly be free, without having to fear the maniac would be released at some point and perhaps come after her again. He was pretty sure her siblings and Jazza echoed his sentiments.

When they were alone again, Jessie quietly asked when he had to go home. "I can stay as long as you need me to. Phillip said he could keep Michael overnight if I need him to. Would you like me to stay tonight?"

"Yes, please." He gave her a quick, light kiss, then called Phillip to let him know about the change in plans. As he hung up, Jessie came up behind him and wrapped her arms around his waist. "Thank you."

He turned, intending to take her into his arms, but she pulled back and turned to go up the stairs. Galen followed as she led him to her bedroom, now finished. As soon as the door closed behind him, Jessie was in his arms, kissing him hungrily, desperately. Knowing she needed an outlet for the complex emotions running through her, Galen gladly met her hunger. They moved back towards the bed, their mouths never parting for more than the briefest of moments. Jessie pulled at the buttons on his shirt, which Galen quickly removed.

When Jessie's knees hit the bed, they paused, each watching the other as they finished removing their clothes. Galen lifted Jessie up on the bed, sitting her on the edge. With her fingers digging into his butt, she pulled him toward her. The bed's height positioned her perfectly for him to slide into her, giving in to her demands. Neither wanted slow lovemaking but took and gave with a raw frenzy. Spent, they crawled up on the bed, lying face to face.

Jessie kissed him, this time gently, slowly. "Galen, I love you."

Galen slid his arms around her and returned her kiss with the same slow, deliberateness. "Good, because I love you too." This time their lovemaking was very slow. They explored one another as if it was their first time again.

In the morning, they lingered in bed until Galen's cell phone alarm rang. Reluctantly, he kissed Jessie goodbye to head back across the street, so he could get dressed for work.

Phillip had already promised to drop Michael off at school. Thinking about his son, Galen realized he should probably have that talk with him soon about his relationship with Jessie, and where Galen wanted it to go.

Chapter 34

ON CHRISTMAS MORNING, Jessie sat sipping hot chocolate as she marveled at the sight of Galen and Michael sitting around the enormous tree they'd helped her pick out the week before and helped her decorate with all the family decorations they'd found in the attic.

Jessie's family was there, as was Galen's brother Phillip. Wrapping paper flew around the room as everyone opened their presents. The adults enjoyed Michael's excitement over the various toys, books, and dog-related goodies he'd received.

When almost all the presents had been opened, Michael grabbed a small box from under the tree and brought it over to Jessie.

"Jessie, this one is for you. I hope you like it."

"Thank you, sweetie, I'm sure I'll love it." Jessie wondered what sort of a present Michael could buy and what might be tucked into such a small box. Under the shining blue wrapping paper, she found a black velvet jewelry box. Opening the box, she gasped, calling everyone's attention to her. Inside the box nestled a white gold ring with a large purple amethyst heart in the center, and two diamond hearts lying on their sides, their tops touching the center.

"Oh, oh, Michael, it's beautiful, I…"

"I really like you, Jessie. You're kind, a good cook, you read me stories and help me with my homework and teach me all kinds of things, and you protected me too." Michael dropped down to one knee as he looked at her. "So, will you please accept this ring and agree to be my second momma?"

"Oh." Jessie's eyes filled with tears at his earnest request. She stole a glance at the grinning Galen. "Well, honey, sure I'd love to be your second momma."

"Really?" Michael beamed. "Oh, I should warn it comes with a catch."

"A catch?"

"Yeah, Dad said that in order for you to be my second mom, you kinda have to marry him. Is that okay?"

"I…I think I can live with being your dad's wife, if he wants me."

"Do I breathe air?" Galen snorted before letting Michael continue.

"Cool, so that's a yes?"

"Yes, that's a yes."

Michael's shout of joy nearly drowned out the sound of the others cheering. He threw his arms around her. Behind him, Galen coughed and pointed to his fingers. "Oh yeah!" Michael quickly helped Jessie removed the ring from the box and slipped it on her finger. "There, now it's official!" He grabbed another hug, before Galen came over to steal a kiss.

"Cute, very cute," Jessie whispered with a smile when they parted.

"Thought you'd like it and figured you should probably have a heads up you were getting double trouble with us."

She laughed and kissed him again, before stroking Michael's head where he hugged her side. "I'd never consider my two favorite guys trouble at all."

James came over to give his sister a hug and a kiss. "Congratulations, Lil' Bit. You've got a good mom there, kid." After tousling Michael's hair, he shook Galen's hand. "Keep her smiling like that and we'll always be good."

Thank You for Reading!

Want to know when my next novel is coming out? Head to my website, SherelleWinters.com to subscribe to my newsletter.

Interested in a behind the scenes look into my stories, my writing career, and being an indie author? Check out my podcast, "The Lackadaisical Writer," available on iTunes, iHeartRadio, Google Play, Stitcher, and more!

Also By Sherelle
(as Anma Natsu)

Aisuru

Deviations

At Week's End

About the Author

Sherelle Winters is an author, podcaster, and software engineer who relocated from her home state of North Carolina to Texas in the early 2000s. Despite her decades in the state, she still longs for good-old-fashioned Carolina-style barbeque versus Texas-style barbequed meats, though she will sometimes admit that she also enjoys good brisket.

A self-professed Japanophile, Sherelle used the country as the setting for her first three novels and notes that her heavy consumption of Japanese media has almost certainly affected her story-telling style and subject matter.

She shares her life with her beloved sweetie, the family she made herself from her closest friends, and her much beloved furkids.

www.ingramcontent.com/pod-product-compliance
Lightning Source LLC
Chambersburg PA
CBHW032123180726
48284CB00002B/682